I0548123

ON HER
GUARD

Protecting Her Series, Book One

BY SKYLA MADI

On Her Guard

Crave Publishing, LLC
Kailua, HI 96734
http://www.cravepublishing.net/

Formatting: Crave Publishing, LLC

ISBN-13: 978-1-64034-268-2
ISBN-10: 1-64034-268-0

NOTE:

On Her Guard was originally intended for a security-themed anthology, but I overshot the word count. I hope you enjoy Ben and Sera's story.

Chapter One

Ben

I suck the last of my chocolate milkshake up the long, red and white straw, uncaring that it makes that annoying slurping sound people hate so much. I feel their stares on me and imagine their eyebrows pulling tightly together as their frustrations mount. The milkshakes are mediocre today. They were the best once. Now I'm not so sure.

I pick up my napkin and swipe it once across my lips before scrunching it in my fist and dropping it into the tall, empty glass. Exhaling, I slide out of the spacious, red leather booth and pull my wallet out of the back pocket of my worn jeans. The milkshakes here didn't always cost five dollars. I swear they hike the price up every time I come back from duty.

Bastards.

I drop a twenty-dollar bill on the table and turn toward the exit.

"See you tomorrow, Ben."

I don't look at the waitress, Donna, as I saunter past the counter where she pours an obese man in a dirty trench coat a fresh, hot coffee.

"See you tomorrow, Donna."

Bells clash together as I press my palm to the door of the isolated little roadhouse on the edge of town and step outside. Fresh spring air on the tail of a gust of wind whips my face and I fill my lungs with it. In the desert, the air never smelled like this.

God bless America.

Stomping down the metal stairs in my heavy, brown boots, I reach into the front pocket of my jeans and pluck out a half empty packet of cigarettes. The packet is a little worse for wear since I've been carrying it around in my back pocket as I jump from job to job. Flicking the cardboard flap back, I pluck out a cigarette and pinch it between my lips.

"What do you want from me, Samantha? Tell me what you want!"

Slipping the packet of cigarettes into my back pocket, I turn toward the ruckus across the parking lot. Car doors slam. *Oh goodie. A milkshake and a show.* I move toward my big black truck and rest against its bull bar, bending my leg at the knee.

"I don't want anything from you!"

"Bullshit!"

The guy comes into view long before the girl does and I light my cigarette as he storms across the lot, gravel crunching underneath his crisp, white sneakers. He tugs his blue letterman jacket together at the front before pushing ten angry fingers through his short, jet black hair.

"I'm not going in there with you if you're going to keep yelling at me!" A short blonde pops out from behind a yellow Beetle, clenching the thick strap to her handbag.

I simper.

"So don't," he shouts over his shoulder as he clears the roadhouse steps in a single bound before disappearing inside.

I drag on my cigarette, watching in silence as she throws her hands up and mutters to herself. I take in her cut-off jean shorts, white halter top, and the belly button piercing that pokes through the slice in the fabric and glistens in the sun. She must be in high school, given her sugary tone and her boyfriend's jacket.

Turning around, she spots me and pauses, eyeing the cigarette in my hand.

"Hey!" she calls out. "Can I get a cigarette?"

I squint as the sun slips out from behind a fluffy, white cloud, its bright light reflecting off the stones. Flicking my cigarette to the ground, I crush it under the sole of my boot.

"Sorry," I say. "Last one."

Of course I'm lying, but I think she knows that. The young girl cuts her eyes at me as I push off my truck and saunter around to the driver's door.

"Fuck you," she snaps, planting her manicured hands on her hips.

My lips quirk. Yep. She's definitely in high school.

I climb into my truck and shut the door. Kids these days feel so entitled. Where I spent my last tour, they'd cut off her head simply because she spoke to me. Again, *God bless America.* This little girl doesn't know how good she has it. Besides, I did her a favor anyway. Smoking is a filthy habit.

I don't smoke often. I've had this packet of mine for a solid month and I'm only now nearing the end. Even though my days no longer leave me trembling with anxiety as the safety of the sun sinks into the horizon, I can't seem to kick the craving for that four p.m. smoke.

The tiny blonde storms toward the roadhouse, not bothering to spare me another glance as I turn the key in the ignition and reverse my truck. The engine's gentle but vicious rumble is music to my ears. I thought she'd sound like shit after my recent eleven-month absence, but she's just as mouthy and glorious as ever, thanks to my neighbor, Josh, who took her around town to stretch her legs every few days.

Vrrrrrrt.

I frown as I pull out of the parking lot and onto the main road. There's another muffled vibration followed by a familiar ringing. I glance down at the center console, but I can't seem to pinpoint where it's coming from. Returning my attention to the asphalt, I turn my radio dial down to hear the ringing better, but the radio is off anyway.

Where the fuck...? Stretching, I reach over the center console and pop open the glovebox. The ringing becomes clear and loud, so I snag my cellphone and answer it.

"Yeah?" I slam my glovebox shut.

"Really, Ben?" my angry little brother snaps. "You quit your job?"

4

"Yeah, I quit," I tell him, moving into the right lane to overtake a light green campervan driving grossly under the speed limit. "Fetching coffees and watching assholes mix cement isn't me."

"It's the first day!" he counters. "You think they're gonna let you pour up an entire driveway by yourself on your first day?"

Frustration bubbles underneath my skin. My brother doesn't understand what I need to survive. I've done four top secret tours throughout the Middle East. *Four.* The last eleven years of my life have been filled with action, blood, violence—hard-*fucking*-work. I've rebuilt entire homes with my bare hands. I've helped construct schools, fix vehicles, and detonate roadside bombs. Hell, I've performed major surgery in the middle of a damn desert to keep a friend alive. There, I had purpose. Here…here I have nothing.

"I've built schools, Declan."

"I know you have, but this isn't the fucking Middle East, Ben. This is the real world! I stuck my neck out to get you this job and you quit before the day is through?" He pauses, and it's lengthy, before finally exhaling. "You were nobody when you first went to the Middle East. You had to work your way up. Same goes here in this country. You gotta *work* for it. No one is going to give you a hand out. They don't give a fuck who you are or what you've done. If they want you to fetch them a coffee, you fetch them a damn coffee."

I lick my lips. Of course, he doesn't understand. I can fetch coffees until the cows come home but, why should I? Why should I have to settle? I'd give anything to be back serving my country. I know it's a horrible life to want to live, but I don't know anything else…and now that Mom's gone, every time I come back here, it feels less and less like home. There's something else missing too, and I can't pinpoint what it is. It's not luxuries. I've bought everything I can possibly want—even a motorcycle that I don't like riding. None of it keeps me distracted long enough to stop thinking about those hot days I spent smoking cigarettes under a makeshift umbrella, my focus never leaving the horizon. I know it doesn't sound like much, but the way my heart raced every time the breeze blew sand off the top of a dune…I never felt so alive…and if I didn't promise my mother on her deathbed twenty-four months ago that I'd stop touring over there and start a life here, I'd go back in a heartbeat.

"Good talk," I mutter, pulling the phone from my ear.

Declan's voice is rushed and unintelligible as I hit the red button to end the call. Exhaling, I toss the phone onto the passenger seat and continue my drive toward the city. It's not often I drive into the city, but someone I know is getting married tomorrow, and the only way I could get out of attending the wedding was to agree to show up at the bachelor's party—which is tonight.

I smooth my hand down the front of my gray tee. I don't look like much, but this is the cleanest shirt I currently own, so it will have to do.

Indicating right, I slip onto the freeway and head toward a bustling Las Vegas.

CHAPTER TWO

Sera

"You be good, baby."

I smile as my father plants a quick kiss on my forehead and nudges me toward the front door. I bat my eyelashes at him, ignoring Leo, who stands on my right, his black eyes burning the skin on the side of my face. "Always."

I pull my long black coat tight around me as I turn and descend the wide, stone steps that lead to the sleek town car waiting for me.

"Keep a close eye on her," Dad says to Leo. "If she gets away from you again…"

I roll my eyes with a smirk as James, my driver, opens my door.

"She won't."

I hear the hard bottoms of Leo's shoes as he storms down the steps and slips into the car behind mine. I glance over my shoulder and wave to my father, who offers one back. I see the warning in his eyes, his threat to punish me if I act out again. Why

7

can't he be a normal father? I'm twenty years old. I don't need an escort—or a guard to watch my every move. It's freaking suffocating. I know he means well, I know he does, but the life he chose for himself shouldn't affect the life I want for me.

Being the only child—and only daughter—of Marco Ventilli, Don of the Las Vegas family, is no walk in the park. You'd think with all this money and power I'd be shitting all over this town, but truth be told, I've barely seen what this town has to offer a young girl like me. I can't break a fingernail without my father finding out about it and I'm at my wits' end. I used to be okay with it all *until* I came of age and wanted to live my life the way my friends did. It's through them that I saw just how trapped I was.

At the age of fifteen, my parents promised my hand to a made man of another family—the Chicago Outfit. I was told I would marry him on my eighteenth birthday and that he'd take my virginity as a gift from my parents. I was mortified by the duties expected of me, so mortified that I took matters into my own hands and gave my virginity to a not-so-nice boy in a dressing room after school when I was sixteen. Why? Because I wanted to do it on my own terms and I didn't want to be in pain on my wedding night. I told my mother about it, hoping she'd praise me for being so clever—or to stop the wedding out of embarrassment at the very least. Instead, she slapped me back to the sixteenth century in a fit of tears. Turns out, it's easy to tell if a girl is a virgin or not and I was in big trouble come my wedding night.

I thought about ending my life as my seventeenth birthday rushed by, but I decided against it since my "husband" was going to kill me anyway and then declare war on my father.

Thankfully, my husband-to-be was shot dead outside his strip club eight months before our wedding and it all went away. It was a fucking miracle. I thought I'd gotten away with it too, until I found out later that it was my father who killed my fiancé. He knew I wasn't a virgin. He told me he knew what I'd done the moment I'd done it, thanks to Mom. I was overrun with guilt at the fact he allowed me to lie to his face and horrified that he let me live with the fear of the consequence of my actions…for *years*. As punishment for what I did, he cut me off from the world even more. For a long time, I couldn't walk the drive to get the mail, but now, after incessant nagging on my behalf, I'm allowed out provided it's under the supervision of a guard. I can't come and go as I please, not until I'm married off and I'm someone else's problem.

I'm getting a little too old for marriage…or so my mother's friends keep pointing out whenever I attend their stupid brunches. Apparently, I'm embarrassing the family, but in all honesty, I don't mind it. I hope I never marry.

Ditching my train of thought, I peer into Leo's car. He watches me intently, his knuckles turning white as he grips the steering wheel. His eyes are narrowed directly at me and I can't help but smile at him. *I have one hell of a night planned, Leo, and you can't stop me.*

I slip into my car and slide along the black

leather seats until I'm sitting dead center. When I'm comfortable, my driver closes the door. In a few minutes, he pulls the car around the elegant, white stone water fountain in the center of our drive and slowly rolls toward the gigantic, wrought iron gate. As he drives, I text my friend Naomi that I'll meet her inside the club in a little under an hour. First, I have to shake Leo. My father thinks I'm seeing a movie with my girlfriends. I showed him fake text messages about the meet up just to prove it too.

I slip out of my plain black flats and open my handbag. Reaching inside, I pull out my favorite pair of Gucci heels and stuff my flats in their place. Slipping into the heels feels like I'm soaking my feet in silk and fucking rainbows. I never want to take them off.

Sighing, I drop back against the leather, smoothing my palms down the length of my black coat. Tonight is going to go one of two ways. One, I get away from Leo, I have a good time, and Leo doesn't say shit to my father about losing me for the second time. *Or,* Leo is going to freak out and tell my father immediately, who'll put a call out and have just about everyone in Las Vegas on the lookout for me. Normally, I wouldn't play with those odds, but I take solace in the fact this will be the *second* time Leo has lost me. He'd rather take his chances turning Vegas upside down looking for me than he would admitting another failure to my father.

It's not long until James pulls the town car in front of the worn movie theatre. I wait patiently while he exits the car and then circles to open the

10

door adjacent the sidewalk. When I get out into the crisp, night air, I glance around.

Nothing.

Excitement boils and bubbles inside me when I don't see Leo's car anywhere. *Could it be?* I start forward and turn away from the wide movie theatre doors, lifting my phone to my face. This turned out to be easier than I thought. James doesn't say anything as I walk down the street toward the main part of town. He doesn't get paid enough to say anything, and the extra pocket money I give him keeps him on my side, not my father's.

"Those shoes are a little dramatic for a screening of *King Arthur*, don't you think?"

I freeze mid-text, my eyes thinning to complete my scowl. *Party pooper.* Slowly, I turn around and there he is. The cock-blocker...or whatever the equivalent is to that in this situation. I bite my tongue at the sight of his smug expression and force an innocent smile.

"It's Charlie Hunnam," I point out, as if it's the most obvious thing in the world. "I'm not wearing flats. What if he's here?"

"I doubt he's here." Leo rolls his dark, espresso eyes and stuffs his large hands into the pockets of his matching pressed slacks. "Where are your friends?"

I slip my phone into the pocket of my coat. "They're already inside."

He regards me curiously. In his stare, I can see him overthinking the situation, trying to predict every single one of my tricks, but there's nothing he can do to stop me from meeting Naomi tonight.

11

Eventually, Leo steps to the side and gestures toward the theatre doors. "After you."

I smile sweetly at him. "Thanks."

As soon as I pass his peripheral, my smile melts into a glare.

Inside the theatre, Leo stands against a far wall while I buy my tickets. For added measure, I buy popcorn, a medium soda, and a bag of sour Skittles. For a moment, I wonder what his plan is, because if he comes into the actual cinema, it's going to be harder for me to get away, and I didn't pack running shoes. Thankfully, after he chats to the ushers, Leo stands right by the door and remains there as I saunter past. My father's men are a lot of things, but stealthy isn't one of them. Leo sticks out like a sore thumb in his fitted black suit and his angry stare.

I smile victoriously when he doesn't follow me and I take a triumphant sip of my Coke before dumping it in the bin provided, along with my popcorn. I stuff my Skittles into my bag as I make my way along an aisle to the front of the room and out an emergency exit. As the door swings open and the bright lights of Vegas burn my retinas, I grin widely.

Sera: one.

Leo: zero.

CHAPTER THREE

Ben

To be honest, I don't go out much.

I sip at my Bourbon and Coke as three women dressed in skimpy, bright pink flamingo bikinis walk by. Unashamedly, I drag my stare all over them. I've been home a while, but I haven't laid a finger on a woman. Not a single one.

When I was stationed in the Middle East, there were women in my platoon. Some of them had families and never crossed any lines, but the other girls there needed to unwind on occasion, like the men did. It was never sordid or dirty, just a couple of adults fooling around. It was a coping mechanism to help us through the weeks as they painfully ticked by.

Most of the women I'm seeing tonight are soft-bodied and curvaceous, unlike the female soldiers I was stationed with. Their bodies were beautiful, sure, but there's something about a woman whose muscles and sharp edges are hidden under seemingly endless miles of soft, curvy flesh that just speaks to me. I like a damsel in distress. I like women who need my large, strong hands to open a jar or to throw them over my—

"Ben!" I whip my head to the left, to Chad, who's the only one in the room I recognize. "Get your ass over here!"

He fraternizes in the middle of the club with a group of girls—young, *young* girls by the looks of it. I'm not picky when it comes to women. I'm attracted to all shapes, sizes, and colors, but age is definitely something I openly discriminate against. I'm thirty-two years old—turning thirty-three in a few months' time. I don't want a girl fresh out of high school or college. Who has time for that kind of drama at my age? The sex might be great, but I bet the conversation is terrible.

I wave him off and sip at my drink, letting it tickle the surface of my tongue for a few long seconds before I swallow. I should go home after I finish. I'm not in the mood. I'm tired as shit *and* I'm uncomfortable—not to mention I'm back to job searching tomorrow. Excusing himself from the gaggle of eager, young women, Chad squeezes his way through the sweaty masses toward me.

"You're killing me here, Ben." He exhales, dropping into the seat beside me.

I laugh. "You don't need my help to get girls."

"Sure, I do. I'm the funny, charismatic, skinny friend who breaks the ice, and you're the brooding, beefy one every girl wants to blow, but they don't have a snowball's chance in hell, so they get with me instead." He swallows a mouthful of beer.

"There's a balance and you're fucking it up."

I roll my eyes. "Where's David?"

"At the slot machines. Should be back any minute with the rest of the gang. He wants to hit the strip club soon, maybe take a few girls back to the hotel." He glances sideways at me, scratching the back of his head. "For the fellas, obviously. Not for him…since he's gettin' married and all."

I shrug. It isn't any of my business what he does tonight—regardless of the fact it's my cousin he's marrying. I don't have any stakes in their marriage, that's for sure. I'm only here for the booze and to avoid going to the wedding. I hate weddings and the invasive questions people feel the need to ask me when I attend them. *When is it your turn? Is there a special someone in your life? You're not getting any younger, Ben.* I take another gulp of my drink and swallow, clenching my teeth.

"I might head off when I finish my drink."

Chad's big, green eyes almost bug out of his skull. "Mate…" he shouts, his Australian accent coming in thick. "You can't head off now. It's still early. Half the clubs in Vegas haven't even opened yet. Not to mention, you haven't seen a single pair of tits."

Tits? I snort. I stopped rating the awesomeness of my night based on how many pairs of tits I saw when I was mid-way through my twenties. These days, if I can leave a club with my dignity intact and *both* my shoes on my feet, I'm happy. Bonus points if I can squeeze in an episode of the British *Top Gear* before bed.

"I'm not in the mood."

"You're never in the mood." He points a slender, nail-bitten index finger at me, gripping his cold beer at the neck with the same hand. "That's your problem."

I clench my glass. Yeah, that is my problem. I can't relate. I want to. God knows my life would be a hell of a lot easier, but I just can't. I know I need to sort out a decent, engaging job, one that doesn't make me want to blow my fucking head off. The rest will come after that.

It has to.

Hopefully, over time, I'll be able to relax a little more. Think less. An easy way to fix my problem would be to head back out for deployment, but I can't do that to Mom. She thought I'd done enough for this country and it was her wish that I leave the military behind me and build a life, get married, and have children. Swept up in the moment—in the grief—I promised her I would, and I'm nothing if not a man of my word.

"Ben! Chad! There you fuckers are!" David, the curly-haired atheist, approaches from the left of the bar with the rest of the guys in tow.

I don't know what my cousin sees in him. Perhaps, if he wasn't so Goddamn rich, she'd be marrying someone else this weekend, someone less…like him.

David and his friends are all dressed the same. In dark denim jeans and formal button up shirts, the sleeves rolled to their elbows, each of them cradling a drink in one hand and a girl in the other. Like a parade of douches. Surprisingly, my brother isn't among them. It's not like Dec to skip a party,

16

especially that of a soon-to-be groom.

"Look who we found," David cheers.

His thin smile falters when he sees me and he immediately releases the blonde, wrapped in a little black dress, from under his arm. Clearing his throat, he nudges her toward Chad and straightens out his shirt.

The blonde slips onto Chad's lap without protest and he stares at me in disbelief, his eyebrows at his hairline.

"That's Naomi," David points out. "The others are Lydia, Chastity, Lilly, Megan, Sasha, Mia, and—"

"Sera!" The blonde on Chad's lap launches onto her tall, red heels without a hiccup and rushes away, leaving Chad to pout like toddler who just dropped his ice cream.

He's a sucker for a girl in a little black dress. When he bags one, he refers to it as his "unicorn." God knows why. Every girl has a little black dress tucked away in the dark depths of her closet.

It's almost sad, watching his wildest dreams come true, only for them to jump out of his lap seconds later. *Almost* sad. I chuckle to myself, finding delight in his disappointment.

In her absence, the group explodes into conversation about what to do next. The sugary giggles and rambunctious laughter is enough to put me off the rest of my drink. Fuck locking myself in a hotel room with these people. I set my drink on the arm of my chair and push myself to my feet. I don't even know why I came here. Crowds make me anxious and the loud noises send chills down my spine. I move away from the group and none of them notice…except Chad, who dives after me like a fucking love-sick Chihuahua. If only he put this much effort in chasing his unicorn in the little black dress.

With a shove, he slips in front of me, cutting me off. "You're not bailing on me."

"I'm tired."

He shrugs his shoulders. "Take a pinger. You'll be fine."

I cut my eyes at him. I'm not taking drugs, and what the hell's a pinger?

"There's a fuckload of girls over there who want to have a good time and bang some sexy bachelors—"

"So—"

"You see the redhead?" He points over his shoulder. "With the red lipstick and the fake tits?"

I don't look. "What about her?"

"She's shopping for some nice blokes to…*you know*."

Chad grins, exposing his white, mostly straight teeth. I watch him, confused as he sticks two straight fingers into a circle he made with his opposing thumb and index finger.

My lips quirk at the corners. "I don't know what you're doing."

He throws his hands up, like *I'm* the idiot. "DP, mate. D-fucking-P."

Sometimes, I feel like I'm friends with excitable college frat boys, not grown ass men. I've done my time. I took advantage of my college years and spent them wisely. Through that experience, I've learned what I like and what I don't like. Sharing a woman with another man? Never again.

"So?"

He feigns insult. "So? Bro, that could be us."

It's not the first time Chad has begged me to partake in something like this, and it's not the first time I've declined him.

Laughing, I push past him. "You're a mess."

"A mess? Ben?"

"I'm not sharing a girl with you, Chad."

"Why not?" he demands, pushing through the crowd beside me. "It's not a gay thing."

I snort. "I'm not the sharing type." I stop and turn toward him. "And there's no way you could keep up with me. I'd only embarrass you."

Chad throws his head back with a hearty laugh. "You'd embarrass me? Bud, I might be half the size of you, but my co—"

"What are you two talking about?" The blonde from before, Naomi, comes out of nowhere and sidles up next to Chad, wrapping her slender arms around his waist. Color me surprised. It seems she's chosen him as her plaything for night. I wonder how he feels about that considering he just prepositioned me for a three way with a redhead.

"Comparing dick sizes, probably."

I turn my head to the sexy, husky little voice that answered Naomi's question on our behalf. I notice her dark copper eyes first, even in the dim lights of the club, and they're striking against the glittering umber that rims both her irises. Her long, dark lashes, their curve perfectly exaggerated with the right amount of mascara, are the cherry on top of

19

her naughty-but-nice look. The girl smirks at me, her plump lips separating enough for me to see a sliver of her white, white teeth. Something inside me tightens at the sight of her, at the sight of her mouth, and it ignites fire deep down in my dormant soul. Suddenly, staying doesn't seem like such a bad idea.

"We were," I state, "and I win."

Pink kisses her cheeks and she looks away, letting her hair fall against the side of her face, working as a curtain between us. I want to push it away.

"Bullshit," Chad protests, feeling the need to defend his junk. "I would out-dick you in length and girth any day."

I laugh. I laugh because I've seen Chad's dick, and while it's not pathetic, it's definitely not worth bragging about.

"Every guy believes his cock is worthy of the name *Mjölnir*, but they rarely come close to striking with all the might of Thor's hammer." The girl's lips quirk as she opens her black coat, exposing a tight, white dress that clings to her tiny, curvaceous body and dips low between her generous bust. "Unless lightning shoots from the sky when you take your cock in your hand, or the earth trembles as thunder roars above you, no one cares what you carry between your legs."

Ha. I quirk an eyebrow. *Creative.*

Folding her coat over her arm, she flicks her long, dark hair over her shoulders.

"I don't have long. Who's ready for drinks?"

"Actually," Chad cuts in, "we're leaving here to

go to a strip joint or two, then probably back to our hotel."

The girl, who I assume is the Sera that Naomi ran after earlier, looks at me. *Really* looks at me, as if she didn't pick me for a stripper-loving kind of guy. I angle my head, trying to get a read on her. The vibes she throws my way are dramatically different than the ones I was feeling before Chad mentioned strippers.

There's disappointment in her stare, rivaled by flares of anger, or is it jealousy? "A strip joint?" she spits, her eyes thinning. "Classy. Have fun with that."

Stepping forward, she snags Naomi by the elbow and pulls her away from Chad. They head for the bar without a glance over their shoulders, like they can find better men to drink with tonight. Un-fucking-likely.

I look at Chad and the expression of confusion and longing on his mouse-like face is almost comical.

"I guess they don't want to go," I say, slipping my hands into the pockets of my jeans. "No surprises there."

They seat themselves at the bar and Sera glances over her bare shoulder at me. Our stares lock and electricity zips over the surface of my skin, inciting goosebumps down my spine. There's a challenge there in her gaze, and I want in on it. There's something about her, something that says, "you can't touch me."

I want to touch her.

I want to completely ruin her for anyone else.

21

Ever.

I swallow hard and she looks away, dipping her head to hide her face behind a curtain of wavy hair. The attraction rapidly forming like a hurricane inside of me comes with a warning siren. It's loud in my ears, deafening even, but I can't work out why.

"Oh, well. We still have the redhead." Chad turns to look at her and his DP-loving redhead is too busy making out with his buddy Shaun to even notice him.

Yeah, I'm not giving up the brunette for the redhead. Not in a million years.

"You've got to be kidding me," he growls under his breath.

I chuckle. Chad never gets lucky. *Ever.* It's not that he's ugly or creepy, it's just…most grown women aren't into men who carry on like a thirteen-year-old boy drinking his first beer. Probably why he hunts for girls in the younger age bracket than his thirty-year-old self.

"You snooze, you lose, pal."

"Fuck off, Ben. This is your fault." He lifts himself onto the tips of his toes and glances around the club. "Where the hell is David?"

I look around the club for David myself, but he's nowhere to be seen. Half of the crew is suddenly unaccounted for. On to bigger and better clubs, I suppose. "It's his last night as a bachelor. He's not going to wait around for us."

"Well, at least we got those two chicks over there."

As intriguing as Sera is, and as badly as I want

my body grinding against hers, I didn't bring my A game tonight.

"*We* don't have anything," I point out, just so we're clear. "*I'm* going home."

"Ben," Chad cuts me off again, this time pressing a hand to my chest. "Come on, man. I need you. Naomi is good to go, but she isn't going to do shit with her friend hanging off her arm being a buzzkill. I need you to keep the brunette busy."

No fucking way. I'm not going to sit around with some girl for God knows how long just so this asshole can get laid.

"Forget it," I tell him, shrugging away from his hand. "I don't babysit."

"I'm not asking you to. All I'm saying is, hang out here with me. I'll buy your fucking drinks if I have to, just give me some to time to work the blonde over as quickly as I can. *Then* you can go home."

I start to decline, but stop when I look at the brunette again. Would it be so bad to get to know her? She doesn't look like trouble, unlike her friend. Sera lifts her freshly poured martini glass to her lips and sips at the clear liquid inside. It'd be a lie if I said those lips of hers don't slay my entire existence. Some men like tits. Others like ass. Me? I like lips.

"Fine," I say. "I'll stay for a few drinks, but if you don't get anywhere by the time I'm finished, I'm out."

His eyes flare with excitement. "Done!"

I follow behind him as he all but dances his way over to the bar. I settle against the glass surface next to Sera as Chad orders himself another beer, plus a Bourbon and Coke for me.

To impress Naomi and Sera, who sit on the tall, stainless steel stools beside us, he orders them another round of drinks too. I eye him sideways. I hope he knows what he's doing. I'd have checked their IDs before buying them anything. I've been stung before, and let me be the first to say, the taller the heels does not mean the older the woman.

Naomi gushes over his generosity, jutting out her small chest as she gently touches his wrist. Chad revels in it, lapping up her sugar like a diabetic housewife, and Sera regards him curiously before cutting her eyes at me.

"What, no strip club?"

Is she giving me sass? "Nah. I'd rather hang out with you."

In the light of the bar, I see her better. She's a flawless creature with a face that could grace any billboard or magazine cover. She quirks a perfectly manicured brow, but she can't keep the bashful smile from curving her lips. "Is that so?"

"Yeah."

I smile at her and color swells in her cheeks, deeper than before. I affect this girl and I like it. Sera leans closer to me, brushing her arm against mine. I'm hyperaware of her touch, her soft warm skin against mine—and that's just her arm. Imagine how the rest of her body would feel pressed tightly against me. I drop my attention to her mouth and she licks her lower lip, making her red lipstick glisten.

"What's your name?"

"Ben."

"Ben," she repeats, brushing something off my shoulder. "I think you're full of shit, *Ben*, and before you commit to wasting your time trying to woo me, I'm not that kind of girl."

Not that kind of girl? I wasn't aware I was pegging her as *any* kind of girl, let alone *that* kind of girl. In fact, her assumption pisses me off. Sera straightens her posture, smug, and the corner of my lips twitch.

"Tell me, what's it like?" I ask.

"What's what like?"

"Tell me what it's like being *so* pretty you automatically assume every man who is nice to you wants to get in your pants?"

"I'm not assuming anything," she protests, cutting her beautiful eyes at me.

Dare I say, she actually looks offended.

"I think you are."

Chad slips between us, nudging me back with his shoulder. "Easy, you two. Let's go to a booth." He shoots me a warning glare over his shoulder. "Would it kill you to play nice?"

"I am playing nice. She—"

"I'm what?" Sera cuts in as she slips off her stool and grabs her drinks.

She has her hands full, her black coat and matching bag still hanging off her arm.

Fine. For Chad's sake, I can play nice. I step around Chad and hold out my hand, offering to take one of her drinks. Pulling her drinks closer to her chest, she tilts her head on the slightest angle and I hate that it's so endearing. "Forgive me if I don't trust a stranger with my drink."

I smirk. She's serious. "I don't need to drug you in order to peel that dress from your body."

Even in this light, I see golden rivers of honey flare in the dangerous depths of her eyes. Maybe I was wrong about her not being trouble. Maybe she's the worst kind.

Naomi chuckles, joining the fray. "I like your confidence, but you're going to need more than that if you want to get between her legs."

First, my confidence is all I've ever needed to get what I want, and second, "Who says I want to get between her legs?"

"Of course you do. Everyone who is *anyone* wants to fuck the daughter of—"

"Naomi," Sera snaps, shaking her head, warning flashing in her eyes. "We're moving to a booth. Are you coming?"

The daughter of who? In Vegas, it's not uncommon to run into someone who's related to somebody big. If I cared enough to know who it was, I'd push for it, but I don't. She's probably the daughter of some mid-level rockstar. There are plenty of those blowing around Vegas.

Pursing her lips, Naomi grabs her drinks and slips from her stool. Unlike Sera, Naomi lets Chad carry one of her drinks, but I don't point it out as I follow Sera around the spacious club. Every now and again, she glances nervously over her shoulder, until she finds us a small booth in the back corner. It's hidden, very hidden, blocked by a large column and a line of people that extends to the bathroom. I frown. Something's up. Either she's underage and she shouldn't be here, or she's hiding from someone.

I sure as hell don't want to stick around to find out.

CHAPTER FOUR

Sera

I wish Naomi never opened her big mouth.

Ben sits across from me in the small booth and I can feel his dark stare on my face as he analyzes me. I know he has no clue who I am because he hasn't come on strong or run the other way, but strangely, he no longer flirts with me. In fact, he looks for any chance to escape, only his attempts are thwarted by his friend Chad who, so obviously and so desperately, wants to bang Naomi. If you ask me, he's trying too hard. She's already decided she's going home with him because he looks "safe." It's just a matter of when.

While Chad talks about his experience in Amsterdam, I take the opportunity to polish off my second drink and pluck my phone out of my bag. According to the time, my movie is set to finish in an hour, and Leo will begin his hunt to save his own ass when I don't come out of the cinema. I figure in an hour's time, I'll text my father and tell him the

28

girls decided on dessert. That will buy me an extra hour or two.

"Getting close to curfew, is it?" Ben's voice, a deep, mellow tone that sends tingles down my spine, startles me and I slip my phone into my bag.

"I'm a grown woman." I smile, drawing all of my anxiety inward, hiding it from my features. "I don't have a curfew."

The lines of frustration on his handsome face smooth into relief. Did he think I was underage? I mean, technically I am, but it's not *illegal* for him to look at me like *that*. It's not illegal for him to touch me like *that* either.

"A grown woman, huh?" He pushes his half-empty glass away. "How old is that?"

"Twenty-five," I lie.

Who cares? It's not like I'll see him again after tonight. Ben surveys me with his dark eyes, trying to find the truth to my words, and I challenge him, keeping my stare locked on his face. The more I look at him, the more I appreciate just how good-looking he is. It's not just one feature that makes him so strikingly handsome either. Everything seems to come together beautifully—his dark eyes, long lashes, full lips, and a strong jaw. I rarely see guys that look like him around Vegas.

"You expect me to believe you're twenty-five?"

A quirk at the corner of his mouth draws my attention. I wonder how his lips move in a wild, passionate kiss or how his large, strong hands will feel as he follows the curves of my body.

He wants to sleep with me. I saw it in his face the first time we made eye contact. I'm not vain, but

I recognize the sudden pause in a man's natural expression when they look at me.

Ben paused.

Ben couldn't keep his eyes on my face.

Lust.

"You can check my ID if you want."

I pray to fucking God he doesn't. He's pondering it, I can tell. Ben strikes me as the kind of guy that requires hard proof and strict organization. I don't know why…maybe it's in the way he sits, like there's a pole in his spine. His jaw is tight and strong and his shoulders broader than the back of a bus. He's the manliest man I've ever seen.

"No. I believe you."

He brushes his leg against mine, sending a tidal wave of electricity through my body. I don't know if it was intentional or accidental, but if my father were here, he'd cut Ben's leg off for touching me. And that's so Goddamn thrilling.

When was the last time I felt the touch of the opposite sex, anyway? It's been so long. What would I even do with him if I did manage to get him alone? I might dress and act like sex is my second language, but it is so far from being true. Ben, however, has this air of indifference about him. He sits in front of me, all proud and mysterious, and I don't think there's a woman in here that could truly blow his mind…but *maybe*, I'm suddenly feeling up for the challenge. I've already made the decision to be stupid and reckless tonight. Why not take it all the way? I've ditched my guard and drank two martinis. After a few shots, I should be good and ready to tackle this…this…fucking beast sitting in front of me.

I lean forward and his eyes flick to my chest. I know the look. It's the look of a man who is *starving* for physical, female attention. Judging the way his gaze runs along the edge of the hemline, two inches from my hard nipples, I'd say he hasn't had pussy in a while. Or maybe he has and he's just weak for another taste.

"Do you want to do shots?" I ask, flicking my tongue over my lower lip, drawing his attention to my face instead of my chest.

He quirks an eyebrow at me and it makes my heart race. I'm going to do some stupid shit with this man. I can feel it in my blood.

"If I did, who'd drive you home?"

What do you know, chivalry isn't dead? I laugh. "I can take care of myself."

The last thing I need is a man dropping me off at my doorstep. He'd be hung by his ankles and drained of his blood by sunrise. No. I'll just call James when I'm ready and he'll do what he's paid to do—drive.

Ben smirks at me and a tendril of excitement wraps around my spine. "All right. Who's going to drive *me* home?"

"You're a big boy." I pluck the toothpick from my martini glass and put it between my lips. "You'll figure it out."

Ditching his conversation about the biggest "bong" he'd ever seen, Chad claps a large hand on Ben's shoulder and the hand I once thought was large practically shrinks in size. "You can stay with me tonight, mate. I booked a suite at one of the places down the road."

Ben grimaces, and even that's a gorgeous look on him. "I'd rather take my chances driving home."

I push myself to my feet and tug down my dress, slipping the fabric further down my thighs. Ben watches, but quickly averts his gaze, pretending the look of my bare skin doesn't kick his heart rate up.

Naomi slips out of the way as I shuffle out of the booth and head to the bar. I don't expect anyone to follow, but the warm presence at my back as I slide my hands along the glass surface of the bar isn't a surprise. I had Ben hook, line, and sinker from the moment we met.

"What do you want to drink first?" I ask, dropping my bag to the floor and propping myself up on a stool.

"That depends." He leans against the bar on his elbow. "Are you drinking to have fun or to get fucked up?"

He looks absolutely mesmerizing in the blue light of the illumined bar. Shadows pool in all of the handsome hollows of his face, the light reflecting perfectly off his short, jet black hair.

"Both."

Grinning, he signals the bartender. "Set up a tab for me. To start, I want six shots of liquid cocaine, please." Tilting his head to the side, his attention is back on me. "Hold on to your heels, Princess. Shit's about to get wild."

***

I hiss and grunt as Ben slams me against the

32

wall, the light switch digging into my spine. Without breaking the kiss, without withdrawing his firm, overpowering tongue from my mouth, he pulls me off the wall and turns sharply, pressing me against the smooth opposing partition in the hall of Chad's hotel room. We're pressed together so tightly, I'm certain there's no visible gap between us. My head spins from all of the shots I took, but I'm hyperaware and super focused on the rough hands that roam my body...

My eyes flutter open and I squint as the warm sun beams through a sliver in the blinds, my gaze unable to focus on anything except the dust that floats so effortlessly through the air. Groaning, I touch my throbbing forehead and roll over, slipping back into unconsciousness.

His large hands are relentless, desperate to feel every inch of me, desperate to get me out of this dress. I gasp as the fabric gives way somewhere below my hips and Ben's hands are right there, pushing the fabric up my thighs.

"I want to taste you," he groans, flicking his tongue along my bottom lip.

He doesn't wait for my agreement. Instead, he plunges his tongue back into my mouth, taking all the air from my lungs. He's a good kisser. The best I've ever had.

Ben doesn't stumble in the dark. He walks confidently, as if he knows where every surface and every stand is situated. Breaking the kiss, he tosses me out of his arms and I squeal as I drop hard against the soft mattress and sink into the blankets. I barely have time to correct my position before he whips his shirt off over his head and drops his body on top of mine, catching himself on his hands either side of my head. The room is dim, but I can make out the shapes of his arms and his chest.

Beautiful.

Every single inch of him…

I open my eyes for a second time, unsure how long it's been since I last did. What the hell is going on? Where am I? I stare at the ceiling, blinking rapidly until it comes into focus. An elegant fan hangs low and spins slowly, casting a gentle breeze against my warm skin. I watch it as it turns, round and round…round and round…

Ben makes me come twice. First on his fingers. Then his tongue. I return the favor, but he stops me with a yank on my hair before he can fill my mouth. He kisses me again and savors his own flavor, groaning into me, as if my saliva were laced with crack. It's obvious in our movements who the most experienced one is. He knows it and I know it, but he leads me well. He puts my hands where he wants me to touch him and I try my best to do it the way he likes, using the noises he makes as a guide. Eventually, when our bodies are damp with clean sweat, he rests against the headboard and pulls me onto his naked lap. In the blink of an eye, his touch turns from desperate and rapid, to soft and sensual. I let my head loll back as he traces the curves of my naked body with his calloused hands. In them, I feel all of his power. He's strong...so strong I'm certain he could crush my bones if he really wanted to.

Ben lifts me, gently, and positions his protected cock at the apex of my thighs, the very tip pushing inside me. I gasp and he holds me steady by the hips, kissing me softly on the lower lip...

Shit.

I shoot up, gathering the knotted, black sheets around my chest. I'm wide awake, no longer dazed by the remnants of last night's shots. I push my dark hair out of my face with one hand and turn to my left. Sure enough, there he is. The man of what I thought were my dreams...

...turns out those weren't dreams at all. They were memories. Of me and him.

Holy fuck. I am in so much trouble.

CHAPTER FIVE

Ben

"What the f—" I jolt awake as the bed shakes violently.

It takes a while for my sight to clear, but when it does, I almost don't recognize my surroundings, until I recall last night and how I got here.

"Shit!" Sera curses, raking her fingers through her long, dark hair as she searches through the mess of pillows and blankets on the floor for her clothes.

She clings to the bed sheet wrapped around her body, hiding it from me, like I didn't lick every inch of it last night. I prop myself up on my elbow with a yawn, ignoring the way my stomach churns. She finds her dress first, hanging off the tall lotus lamp by the window, and she snatches it up along with her white panties. I watch in amusement. I don't know why she's so flustered. This was *her* idea. I told her no, but she begged and begged and *begged*. The shit she was saying was impossible to ignore. Not to mention, she put my hand between her legs

36

when it was just us alone at the booth. I slipped my finger underneath the hemline of her panties and touched her soft, wet flesh. That was the moment my resolve went out the window. I tried to nail her right then and there. She was all over me. Her sexy mouth on mine, her teeth snagging my lower lip. I would have too—and she would have let me—if Chad hadn't interrupted and coerced us into coming back to the suite he hired out.

"I'm so fucked," Sera utters under her breath as she storms into the bathroom and slams the door behind her.

My lips quirk at her unintended implication. A few minutes later, she returns with her clothes on, her dress noticeably torn, and her handbag in her hand.

"Where are my heels?" she asks, pulling her black coat around her and tightening the belt around her waist.

All the make-up she was wearing last night has long since been removed and she looks just as captivating. At some point during the night, I told her she was the most beautiful woman I'd ever seen. Good to know the light of the morning hadn't turned me into a liar.

I shrug at her. "I told you to hold onto them."

Her eyes are narrow, and cold as if I'm the enemy. They flash with resentment and anger, mimicking lightning on a pitch-black night. "Shut up, Ben."

Raking her fingers through her hair for a fourth time, she glances around the room, seeking her shoes. I frown at the look of actual panic on her face as she opens her handbag and plucks out a black pair of flats and tosses them to the floor.

"I take it sharing breakfast before we go our separate ways isn't happening."

Slipping into her shoes, she shakes her head.

"Is everything okay?"

"Peachy." She marches toward the door.

"Sera?"

Without a glance over her shoulder, she slams the door behind her and I'm left staring at the dark, lacquered wood like an idiot. It's safe to assume last night is something she definitely regrets. God knows why. It was *her* idea. I drop back against my pillow with a heavy exhale and the door is thrown open again.

"You dirty dog!" Chad hollers, bouncing in with a cup of coffee.

I cringe at the loudness of his voice as it rings through my ears, the pain burying itself behind my eyes. I grab Sera's pillow and pull it over my head, not wanting to hear another word come out of his mouth or see his naked torso.

"Ah, come on, Ben. Don't be shy."

The mattress compresses as he climbs on and snatches the pillow. I squint up at him.

"I'm naked under here," I point out. "Get off the bed."

He shrugs and holds out the mug. "Don't worry about it."

The smell of instant coffee flows into my nose and it reminds me of the shit we drank in the desert. It's funny, this situation. A hangover is how I met Chad originally. We were both touring in the same place and one night, during my rostered week off, I had a little too much to drink. I woke up on top of a dune underneath a shitty little sail with Chad towering over me, a weak cup of coffee in his hand and a stupid ass grin on his face. Our friendship blossomed from there.

We weren't stationed together often. I spent most of my time at a different base, but we always got along whenever we were in the same place. He blew his knee out in an incident three months into his second deployment. The vehicle he was driving grazed a roadside bomb. I heard two others didn't make it, but Chad did. We lost contact for a while because I was still in the military while he recovered, but I ran into him again at Sonnie's diner years ago. After that, he moved to Vegas and never looked back.

Propping myself up, I take the mug and swallow a large mouthful of the lukewarm liquid, trying not to be bothered by Chad's green, wide-eyed stare.

I frown with a swallow. "What?"

"She did not look happy. What'd you say to get her to leave?"

"I didn't say anything. She woke up in a panic and ran."

"Maybe you're not as handsome in the light of the morning as you are under the neons."

"Ha. Ha." I feign amusement. I don't even want to talk about it. Nothing damages your confidence quite like a girl sprinting from your room at the sight of you in the morning. "How'd your night go?"

Chad's excitement deflates from his chest and

wipes the smile from his face. "She drank too much. I spent most of this morning holding her hair back while she puked."

I laugh. How could I not? Like I said, he has the shittiest luck when it comes to women and sex. I thought he had Naomi in the bag. I mean, he could have, but he's too much of a nice guy to take advantage of a woman who's not in her right mind.

"She still here?" I ask, taking another sip of my coffee.

"Yeah. She's in the kitchen." He scratches at his disheveled hair and pushes off the bed. "I should go check if she needs more water."

I turn and set my unfinished coffee on the bedside table. What's the time, anyway? I have to go and get started on that job search. Like my late father always said, there's no honor in laziness.

"You're not going to stay?" Chad asks, lingering at the door. "We can hit Sonnie's up for some breakfast or—"

I shake my head. "Can't, sorry. I've got to find a job."

I don't even want to think about how much money I spent last night. Shots don't come cheap, and those fucking bartenders know how to take advantage of people who are too wasted to keep track of what they're spending. Chad leans against the doorframe, frowning at me while I hug the sheet to my hips and bend over the edge of the bed for my jeans.

"What about Terry? You gonna give him a call?"

I don't look up as I slip my legs into their respective holes. "Who's Terry?"

"My boss. I gave you his card last night. You said you were gonna hit him up for a job."

I pull my jeans to my knees and stop. Chad works in private security, but he doesn't do much due to his bad knee. Injury or not, I'm not the kind of guy who can sit around staring at a computer monitor, waiting for movement.

"Me? In private security?" I scoff, sliding my jeans further up my legs without exposing my junk. "No thanks."

Chad turns around, giving me my privacy. "Why not? It's easy, you get a gun sometimes, and, if it's really quiet, you get to sleep on the job."

"I'm just not looking for that kind of job. I want..." I stand up and pull my jeans into place before zipping the zipper. "I don't know what I want."

"Well, if you're looking for something more exciting, Knox Private Security does armored vehicle cash collections, offers security for celebrities, and a whole bunch of other shit. Terry would snatch you up."

I walk around the room, looking for my shirt. *I know I tossed it somewhere...* "I'll think about it."

I find my shirt by the leather armchair against the far wall. When I pick it up I uncover Sera's heels. I stare at them for a second, contemplating what I should do. I could take them to her...

...but on second thought, I'd rather not.

I pull my shirt over my head and smooth my palms down the front, unable to rid the fabric of its wrinkles. Chad disappears while I gather my socks and shoes and put them on, but I find him again in

41

the kitchen, sitting with Naomi, who's seen better days.

She hunches over a cup of coffee in nothing but Chad's shirt from last night. As I pass, she offers me a small smile, but it quickly fades with the obvious turning of her stomach.

"Let me know if you call Terry," Chad shouts as I drag my tired ass down the hall, toward the front door.

"Will do."

I grab the handle and tug the door open, stepping out into the corridor. No one else stirs in the hotel and I'm glad I won't have to share the elevator with anyone on the way down. As I walk, I glance at all the trimmings and adornings, not remembering any of them from last night.

Good. It makes it that much easier to forget.

***

I spend the next forty-eight hours walking around Vegas, trying to find a job, and there's nothing that suits me. My brother thinks I'm being childish by not settling for anyone that will take me, and maybe I am, I don't know. I just...I just feel like I have to at least enjoy my job if I'm giving up the only one I've known and loved. Is that too much to ask?

At the end of the second day, when all I could find were jobs in ice cream parlors and strip clubs, I decided to bite the bullet and give Terry a call. It went smoothly. In fact, Chad had already talked me up and Terry didn't even want an interview...

…which brings me to now.

I stand by Darius, who pulls stacks of cash out of his bag and fills up the ATM machine. This is the third ATM machine we've filled on our morning run, and each and every one has been as uneventful as the last…which I guess is good. Darius doesn't seem like the kind of man that can handle anything dramatic.

I plant my hands on my hips and drag my index finger over the lock to the heavy gun in my holster. God, it feels good to have this bad boy on me—and it's not just the gun that has me well and truly in my comfort zone. It's my uniform. Everything is crisp and somewhat stiff, like a fresh pair of fatigues. My khaki button up shirt is snug, yet breathable, and my forest green pants are tight around the ankles and tucked into my big, black boots.

Yep. Almost feels like home.

The click of high heels to my left draws my attention like a dog to a bone, and a young, slender woman in a tight, black pantsuit approaches quickly, her attention focused only on the cell she holds in her hand. I don't say anything as she closes in on the perimeter I set up in my head. In eight more steps, she'll breach the distance I've set for Darius's safety.

…*six*
…*five*
…*four*
…*three*
…*two*

"Excuse me, ma'am." I step forward, cutting her off, and she startles to a halt, clenching her chest.

"Oh, my goodness." She chuckles nervously, pushing short, walnut locks out of her face. "You scared me."

"Sorry. Didn't mean to scare you." I extend my hand to her and she glances at it. "I just need you to step back a little so my coworker can safely finish his job."

"Of course." She slips her manicured hand in mine and I guide her around my invisible perimeter. "I'm so sorry. I didn't see you two."

Her gaze flicks between my eyes and my lips as she walks, and I wonder if she ever watches where she's going. If she's not careful, she's gonna end up hurting herself.

I release her on the other side. "Thank you very much for your cooperation. Have a nice day."

The woman glances over her shoulder with a gentle grin. "I will."

I watch her walk away and I know she's swinging her hips like that just for me. She sure as hell wasn't walking that way before she knew I was here. I watch her, unashamedly, as she rounds the corner and disappears. A large hand clamping down on my shoulder pulls me from my thoughts.

"You're a real ladies' man, aren't you?" Darius chuckles.

I shrug, grinning as he closes up the ATM machine and pulls his empty cash bag onto his shoulder. "Nah."

I walk beside him toward the truck.

"For future reference, you're supposed to set a *physical* perimeter so people know where they can walk and you won't have to talk to nobody."

"Oh. Right."

I don't mention to him that I haven't actually been trained. Darius's usual partner called in sick—late notice—and Terry threw me in last minute. All he said was *"drive the truck and watch Darius's back."*

For the most part, this job seems pretty straight forward, but there are a lot of fucking protocols I'm supposed to know about, and my official training period doesn't start until next week.

Darius nudges me in the ribs with his elbow. "You'll get the hang of it."

He reaches for the passenger handle and the truck roars to life. What the fuck? Darius looks at me and all I can do is stare back at him, wide eyed, like an idiot.

"Tell me you didn't leave the keys in the truck."
Fuck.

The truck jerks forward, tugging Darius a foot before he lets go.

"Shit!" he shouts, plucking his radio off of his shoulder. Behind me, he shouts gibberish into the line, demanding that the paint be detonated and the police notified. The truck slowly picks up speed and I see it getting away. Are we supposed to wait? What the fuck did they give me a gun for then? My fingers twitch and my blood ignites at the thought of taking matters into my own hands. Would I get in trouble? Could I get in trouble?

Fuck it.

I take off, sprinting down the sidewalk like a mad man, ignoring Darius's shouts behind me. I pull my gun from my holster and hear the gasps and squeals of people around me. It all happens so fast, my surroundings blurring as if I'm running faster than the speed of light, my target the only clear thing in my line of sight.

I clear benches without thought, shooting myself into the air and landing with a swift roll. As the truck takes a left, I hear police sirens in the distance, and if I'm going to salvage this, I need to get to the truck before they do.

A large crowd exiting a classy café blocks the sidewalk and I make the last-minute decision to dive onto the cars parked along the side of the road. *I hope Terry has insurance.* Metal bends and compresses under my heavy boots as I sprint along the roofs of the cars. One by one, I dent them with my weight, but I can't stop. As I reach the end of the street, I see a bus approaching out of my right peripheral and I know I'm not going to be able to pass it in time.

So I take my shot.

I pull my hand gun up and straighten my arms. I close one eye, but it doesn't help. I line up the back-right wheel, hold my breath and pull the trigger.

A shot rings out and energy from the round kicks into my hands. It vibrates up my arms, tickling my skin in the most delicious of ways. I inhale as the hairs on the back of my neck stand up and the nerves down my spine dance. I adjust my position as the truck begins to swerve out of control and I pull the trigger again, hitting the left tire.

The long, yellow bus I was expecting passes me and I wait, catching a glimpse of myself in the reflections of the windows. For the first time in months, I finally look like myself. The bus rolls by just in time for me to see the perp dive out of the driver seat and crash to the ground. His hood falls into his face as he hits the asphalt and rolls six feet.

I'm off the roof of the black car and sprinting toward him before I even have time to register what the fuck I'm doing. I should let the police handle it, but I'm still driven to go for that citizen's arrest. I need it. This is the most exciting thing to happen to me since...since...forever. I feel myself smile as I run, closing the distance between myself and the man who thinks he can steal from me.

He scrambles to his feet fairly quickly, but I've already found my stride. I re-enter the sidewalk as traffic becomes congested. I push chairs out of the way and demand people move before I plow through them. A group of men in suits don't listen to me and they're thrown aside as I come through like a freight train.

I'm only six feet away from the thief now. He's skinny, and young. He glances over his shoulder and he's fucking terrified when he sees me. I contemplate shooting him in the shoulder, but change my mind since he's just a kid, surely no older than eighteen.

The kid tries his hardest to outrun me, but he's quickly losing breath. I've run miles through the desert for days. I could run this entire city without collapsing.

He's four feet away now and I take the dive. The kid grunts as I crash into him, tackling him to the ground. The skin of my elbows catch the rough sidewalk and I clench my teeth as it eats away my flesh when we slide.

"A for effort, kid," I pant, lifting myself off him to plant a knee against his spine.

"Fuck you."

I grab his arms and pin them behind his back before handcuffing them in place. Exhaling, I pull the perp to his feet and drag him over to the nearest café, moving him out of the sun. Cops approach then and they take him out of my possession, demanding I sit and wait for them to take my statement.

A waitress at the small-time café brings me out a jug of water and some sliced orange while I wait. I reach for the jug, only to stop when the suited men from earlier approach, their shoulders squared, their dark eyes threatening.

I expect one of them to speak, at the very least, but they don't. Instead, they step to the side—*very* dramatic like—and up strolls an older, rounder gentleman. He smooths a chubby hand over his round belly, seemingly straightening out his white, button up shirt. He looks like a tourist with his pressed, black slacks, leather shoes, and shiny Ray-Bans that hide his eyes, but I don't think he is. No. There's something too…*comfortable*…about him.

The man doesn't say anything as he lowers himself into the chair across from me. I contemplate opening my mouth first, but decide against it. This is Vegas and this man could be anybody.

"Quite a show you put on," he says, breaking the silence.

His voice is deep and rough, straightening my spine. It's the kind of voice that sends alarm bells ringing in my head, the kind of voice every movie villain conveniently has. I glance over his exterior, not focusing on anything besides the graying hair at his temples.

"Just doing my job," I say, peering out into the street as the cops work on freeing the traffic out of gridlock.

My phone vibrates over and over in my pocket, but I ignore it. It's probably Terry ready to go postal on my ass.

"You're confident *and* competent with your gun."

"I'm a soldier," I say with a shrug. "Or was...I *was* a soldier."

"I could use a *soldier* like you for a special job I need done."

I glance at his men and they all watch me intently. By the looks of them, I get the feeling their boss isn't asking. Ah. It suddenly all makes sense. These guys are a part of the mob. The suits, the silence, the intimidation game. Five bucks says they're all carrying. If I'm right, if they are a part of the mob, the man sitting across from me is none other than Marco Ventilli.

I've seen him and his men around Vegas from time to time. Now, I'm no casino rat or strip club fiend, so my interactions with the mob have always been minimal, but I know they're not the type of people I should fuck with.

"With all due respect, I don't do those kinds of jobs," I tell him.

I bounce my knee as my nerves get the best of me. How do you turn down the mafia without pissing them off?

"What makes you think it's one of *those* kinds of jobs?"

I lean closer. "You're in the mob, right?"

He doesn't agree nor disagree and I take it as my answer. I'm not going to go from fighting for my country to working for the mob. What does that say about me? It goes against everything I stand for. I fight *against* terrorists. I fight anyone who wants to do this country harm. I don't join them.

"Why don't you sleep on it and join me at my place for breakfast tomorrow morning to discuss the position."

Again, he doesn't pose it as a question. He pushes his chair back and the metal scrapes against the cobblestone sidewalk. I open my mouth to decline, but he cuts me off with the point of his finger.

"I'm being patient with you, soldier," he bites out, whipping off his sunglasses. "Don't deny my generosity a second time."

I grit my teeth at the sight of his eyes. There's something awfully familiar about the dangerous flare of gold amongst the brown, but I don't think we've met before.

I can't turn him down. Not for something as simple as breakfast, anyway.

"I'll see you at breakfast."

They look like they're about to leave as a policewoman approaches me in her khaki uniform, notebook in hand, but decide to stay. "They're not giving you any trouble, are they?"

I shake my head. "No, ma'am."

She lowers her sunglasses to the slope of her nose, watching me with curious azure eyes. "What do they want?"

"To congratulate me," I lie. "On catching the bad guy."

"Is that so?" She pushes her glasses up her nose. "You've broken a few laws today, Mr...?"

"Campbell." I scratch at the back of my head. "I was just doing my job."

"Your job is to fill ATM machines, *not* open fire on the public."

Is she kidding me? He would have gotten away if I didn't stop him. "I didn't *open fire* on the public. I prevented a carjacking and a lot of money being stolen."

"Who's your superior?" Marco cuts in, stuffing his hand into his pocket.

He speaks with fire in his tone. He couldn't care less that woman in front of me is wearing a badge.

Straightening her top, the officer clears her throat. "Paul Hendrix."

"Paul, huh? Well, you tell Paul that if he has a problem with our boy here, then he has a problem with me."

"*Your* boy? This has nothing to do with you," she grinds out, her blonde eyebrows disappearing under the metal of her glasses.

"Of course it does." Marco flicks a finger at me. "He's with us. Aren't you, Ben Campbell?"

What the hell is happening right now? I glance between Marco and the officer. Both of them watch me, pulling me in two. Do I take my chances with the law and take the penalties on the chin? Or do I side with Marco and risk…well, everything? Marco has put me in a tight fucking spot and he knows it.

"Yeah," I say, the excitement I'm supposed to feel not quite reaching my voice. "I'm with them."

The police officer is glaring at me through her sunglasses, I just know it. "My superior will be in touch with you."

She whirls on her heel and storms away. Just like that.

I knew when I drew my gun from its holster that there might be consequences, but I did it anyway and now—all of a sudden—I'm involved with the Las Vegas mafia and the police can't touch me? What the hell happened in less than an hour?

"Breakfast," Marco states, tossing a card onto the table as he turns away. "Oh-eight-hundred, soldier. Don't be late."

Don't be late.

Code for: *I'll cut a finger off for every minute you keep me waiting.*

CHAPTER SIX

Sera

I roll over onto my back and stare up at the ceiling. My eyes feel like ten-pound stones sitting in my sockets and my stomach churns painfully, running on nothing but coffee fumes and a quarter of a peanut butter bagel that I had for dinner last night.

When I finally made it home after my naughty little rendezvous with Ben, boy, did shit hit the fan. I'd never seen my father so angry—and I can't forget my mother. She was hysterical, crying about me lying face down in a ditch somewhere. I came up with the best story I could, but nothing sufficed. My guard, Leo? He never came back. I didn't count on him being too much of a pussy to face my father. Whatever punishment he *was* going to face will be a million times harsher now that he's abandoned his post.

I lied to my parents about driving to a diner out of town with Naomi and her car broke down. I spun a tale about walking miles and miles back to her house and it being too late to come home. I pushed most of it onto Leo since he wasn't coming back, claiming he abandoned us, and I even went as far as to wipe my phone and give it to a homeless man on the street.

Of course, Dad didn't believe a word I said. He slapped me across the face and called me all kinds of names. Now here I am...twenty years old and grounded. I'm not allowed to leave the house for anything.

I'm a fucking prisoner.

I'm not going to lie, though. It was worth it. That one night...God, I had the best time, and Ben? He was incredible. I'm almost kicking myself for not getting his number. I would love to see him again.

Sighing, I kick off the blankets and push myself out of bed. As I sit on the edge, I glance around my room. Long gone are the days when my space was filled with fluffy toys and glitter. Now my room looks like it belongs to a certified adult, so why do they insist on treating me like a child? I'm not buying into the whole "mafia" shit either. I know tons of girls with fathers who are made men and they get to do whatever the hell they want...but not me. Never me.

I lift myself onto my feet as I push my fingers through my hair and cross the soft carpet to the door. Outside in the hall, there's no movement. Usually, Loretta is cleaning the cinema room by the time I wake up, but not this morning, which means one of two things. One, she's not working today, or two, she's helping out in the kitchen. Loretta is the only one in my father's staff who knows how to make a mean cavolo nero and fontina piadina, and if she's making that...my father must have guests.

I make my way down the hall, uncaring that only a thin, white tank top covers my bare breasts and the tiniest pair of bed shorts cover my ass. Normally, I'd put on a dressing gown to avoid a lecture, but the sun is out and the air is crisp and warm, meaning my father will be entertaining in the courtyard by the pool.

No one lifts an eyebrow at me as I enter the kitchen, except my mother, who stands by the far window, watching whatever is going on outside.

"Come here, child," she spits, taking in my pajamas as she shrugs out of her light pink dressing gown. "Your father will have a heart attack if the men see you like that."

I glance down. Like what? It's not like I'm going to pour water down my torso or jump into the pool. If they get excited because of a tiny point in my shirt, then that says more about them than it does about me.

I blow impatiently out of my nose as she pulls her gown around my shoulders. I slip my arms in and she closes it up, tightening it around my waist. Mom and I are very much the same size. Often, we're mistaken for sisters. We both share long, dark, wavy hair, and a slender frame. However, where her eyes are a beautiful olive green, mine are borderline black with tiny flakes of honey, like my father's.

"What's Dad doing, anyway?" I ask, knowing I'm probably not going to get a straight answer.

She turns back to the window, slipping a manicured nail between her top and bottom teeth. "Interviewing a new guard for you."

I roll my eyes, suddenly not interested in whatever is going on in the courtyard. "Why not use someone who already works for him?"

I turn toward the fruit platter on the bench and pluck a grape from the top. I squeeze it between my thumb and forefinger before slipping it between my lips.

"He needs all of his men for something else." She inches closer. "He seems to really want this...this...Ben guy, but he has no experience."

I pause—mid-chew—and swallow the grape. Did she say Ben? Or did I hear Ben? I clear my throat as dread creeps into my chest, nice and slow. "Who?"

"His name is Ben Campbell." Mom says, not taking her eyes off the courtyard. "Your father found him downtown yesterday, jumping over cars and shooting the wheels off a truck."

I frown, a lot relieved, and a little disappointed. That doesn't sound like my Ben at all.

Not that he's *my* Ben. He's not.

I close the distance between Mom and I and peer out into the courtyard. I see my father's wide back first and he's hiding whoever is sitting in front of him, until he leans to the side to grab his prima colazione. I gasp loudly at the sight of short, jet black hair and the broadest pair of shoulders I've ever seen. What the fuck is he doing here? Did I tell him who I was? Does he think this is a fucking game? My father and his men would skin Ben alive if they knew what we did.

I hate that I think he looks incredible in a tight, white button up shirt with the sleeves rolled to his elbows, exposing deliciously thick forearms. I also hate that the top button is undone, exposing his throat and the very top of his chest, but...*damn*...the guy knows how to dress for an interview.

"I don't like him," I mutter, clenching the edge of the table in front of me.

"Your father's counting on it," Mom replies with a gentle quirk of her lips.

I have to go out there. I have to put a stop to this. I turn on my heel and rush out of the kitchen toward the back door, ignoring my mother as she snaps my name between her perfect teeth.

Ben

"The thing is..." I start, trying to tiptoe my way around offending Mr. Ventilli, who's gone out of his way to prepare this incredible spread just for our meeting. "I've never had to guard someone before. I've never had to follow someone around town and make sure they stick to curfew. That's not really me."

He sits back in his chair, lifting his cigar from its ashtray. "I'm not looking for experience. I'm looking for skill, and you have plenty of that."

I glance around at the men surrounding us. They stand quite a few feet away and they don't look at us, but I know they're listening. Why can't he use one of them? Why me?

"I can shoot a gun, but I can't—"

"—I'd make it worth your while," Marco cuts in, tapping a chubby finger against the arm of his chair. "Pay you more money than you've ever seen in your life."

My eye twitches. Money would help influence my decision. I don't want it to, but it'd help pay off my mother's house. I snap myself out of my money-induced stupor. Money isn't shit when you're dead. What if something happens to the girl on my watch? What if I fail? They'll cut my head off.

I clear my throat and shift on my seat. "The risk is more than the gain. What happened to the last guard?"

"If you want information, you have to be a part of the family." He spits a tiny piece of his cigar from his lip. "Do you want information?"

"I…"

Truth be told, I need a job. Terry fired me on the spot—fucking ridiculous since I hadn't undergone any official training. He said the cops are on his ass with an investigation now and he'll probably lose his job. It seems since Marco made it so law enforcement couldn't come after me, they went for Knox instead, and the company itself is facing a massive fine. I couldn't argue with the guy, not really, so I took the termination and I left without protest. My brother called me two hours later after seeing shit on the news. The whole ordeal has been a damn mess, but no media and no police have come for me…because of Marco. I know that's not a good thing, but what am I to do? At this point, I kind of owe the guy. If I leave here without taking this job, who knows what's waiting for me on the other side of his stone wall.

"Okay…" I say, nodding. "I'll—"

My words are caught in my throat as the huge double doors to the back yard open and out steps a—*oh, I don't fucking believe this*. My eyes bug out of my damn skull at the sight of her. *Sera.* The girl from the other night.

Oh, fuck. This is not happening. She marches toward us, her pink gown splitting at the front, exposing one long, smooth leg and a sexy thigh that I licked all over. I clench the arms of my chair in my hands and look away. I pray to God she's not his wife. My lungs tighten in my chest and I reach out for my orange juice, taking a sip for the first time since it was presented to me. I guess that explains why she bailed first thing the morning after.

I feel the stares of Marco's men on me, gauging my reaction to the woman approaching. I force myself to relax and glance out over the pool, seemingly uninterested even though every muscle in my body is coiled tightly.

"Morning, Daddy."

Erhg. I take another sip of my orange juice to hide a gag-slash-gulp. I don't know if she's using that word in a kinky way, or if he's actually her father. What's worse? At this point, they both end up with me getting shot. Sera kisses Marco on the cheek and stands beside him, cutting her dark eyes at me.

She drops her head back and I kiss her damp

neck, brushing my thumb against her collarbone. Sighing, she pushes her fingers through my hair and squeezes the strands in her fists. With a rough tug, she forces my face to hers and devours me with a greedy kiss as she grinds her pelvis against mine, forcing our bodies together.

I snap myself out of it, still gobsmacked, as the gentle breeze blows her long hair against her face, but she doesn't bother swiping it away.

"This is my daughter," Marco states, looking down his nose at me. "Seraphina."

"Sera," she cuts in, touching her father's shoulder. "I prefer Sera."

Now I know why Marco's eyes are so familiar to me. They're exactly like his daughter's.

His. Daughter's.

I'm relieved that she isn't his wife, but *very* fucking nauseated that she's his little girl. If he *ever* finds out…declining this job will be the least of my worries.

I lick my lower lip out of nervousness. "So, she's the job then?"

I should never have come here. I should have ended this at the cafe.

"Don't let her pretty face fool you, Ben Campbell. I go through guards like I do underwear. The girl is a handful."

Oh, I know she's a handful. She's a handful and a half. I don't look at her. I keep my eyes on Marco and pretend she's not standing right behind him. I pretend she doesn't exist.

"I can't do it, Mr. Ventilli." I exhale as I lean

back in my chair. "I've never done it before. Doesn't that concern you?"

He leans forward, resting his elbow on the table. "Let's cut to the chase. You know who I am, you know what I do, correct?"

"I have an idea."

"So, you understand the kind of dangers my family has to face?"

I nod.

"I'm more concerned about someone kidnapping my daughter while I'm not there to protect her than I am about whether or not you can stand in one spot for hours while she shops. You're confident with a gun, your fitness level is above par, and you're not afraid to get shit done in the public eye." He places his cigar in the ashtray. "That's why I want you. I trust you with my daughter and I don't know you from a bar of soap. How about you show me the same in return."

He shouldn't trust me—not with his daughter. Not with the girl I've already defiled in lots, and lots of different ways. To take this job would be an insult to him.

I peer at Sera, who regards me with wide eyes filled with warning. She doesn't want me to take the job. Can't she see that I don't want to take the job either, but my hands are tied?

"Milo would make a good guard," Sera chimes in. "He's capable."

"This doesn't concern you," Marco says, not turning to look at her. "You're the reason Ben and I are having this conversation." Sera clenches her jaw and looks out across the yard. "If you're going to be out here, you'll keep your mouth shut while the grown men talk or I'll ground you for another week."

Jesus Christ. The way he used the term "grown men" has me sweating. This keeps getting worse and worse. Grounding? She's grounded? How fucking old is she? I'm assuming she's not twenty-five, like she said. My stomach turns. Fuck. *Please be older than eighteen.* She has to be. Her body…there's no way she's younger than that.

"I'm not a child," she bites out, pushing away from her father's chair.

"You are as long as you live under my roof," Marco shouts after her before turning his sights on me. "Don't have kids. More stress than they're fucking worth."

I chuckle nervously. "How old is she?"

Please, be older than eighteen. Please be older than eighteen. My feet warm up in my shoes. I can almost feel the heaviness of concrete chained to my ankles already.

"Seraphina? She's twenty."

Oh, thank God. My relief is short-lived. Twenty is still a hell of a lot younger than what I'm comfortable with. She lied to me.

"What's it going to be, Ben? I don't have all day."

He shifts uncomfortably, reaching for something in the waistband of his pants. With a heavy hand, he places a handgun on the surface of the table and I hear the threat loud and clear. Either he's only trying to intimidate me or I'm not leaving this house alive. I'd say my odds are fifty-fifty.

62

"All right." I say, regretting it the second the words come out of my mouth. "When do you want me to start?"

A devious grin plays on the lips of my new boss. "In exactly two weeks. Six a.m. sharp." Standing up, he reaches into his pocket and pulls out a small set of keys. "You'll stay in the guest house while you work for me until further notice."

I didn't realize I'd be a live-in bodyguard...but I guess it's too late to dispute that now. I glance over my shoulder. The large stone guest house is an entire house in itself. I don't think it's a good idea for Sera and I to stay on the same grounds, but what can I do? It's not like I can fight him.

"Okay."

"Stay for the food if you want. I've got work to do."

He walks off and his men follow, some breaking off to play a game of pool under the large awning to the left of the house. I sit for a while, watching.

What the fuck have I gotten myself into?

CHAPTER SEVEN

Ben

Two weeks later

I feel like an idiot, dressing the way they want me to. I straighten my black sports jacket and undo the top button of my white formal shirt. Apparently, it's important to Marco that people know who I work for just by looking at my outfit. I feel like I'm going to some elegant event instead of guarding some girl on a night out with her friends. How do they expect me to do anything in these black slacks and leather shoes? What if I have to chase her? Or climb a fence? These shoes provide no grip—or at least, not the kind of grip I'm used to.

I'm hoping, when I prove myself, they'll let me dress more my speed and less theirs.

According to Marco, he's putting Sera through a test tonight. He's letting her go to any one of his nightclubs, provided she doesn't drink and stays where I can see her. It's a test for me too. That's why he's making me watch her in a place where he has eyes everywhere. If I fuck up...I bet I'm done for.

I follow her through the halls of her house, her heels clicking against the white marble floors. We haven't spoken yet—not since the night we spent together—but I've put a lot of thought into what I want to say to her the minute we're alone, and none of it is pretty. Judging by the way she's been glaring at me from across the room all day, I'm gonna guess what she has to say isn't nice either.

Sera walks fast to get away from me, but my strides are bigger than hers and I manage to keep her in my sight the whole way to the front door. She looks absolutely breathtaking in a cute red party dress with a flirty sweetheart neckline that draws attention to places I wish it wouldn't.

When she entered the backyard while her father briefed me on what to expect earlier tonight, my gaze roamed her entire body of its own accord. From her black heels to her elegant hair bun, I completely devoured her. Unimpressed, Marco jabbed a finger into my chest and said: "Watch her, but don't watch her. If I ever catch your stare lower than her face, I'll have them ripped from your skull."

All I could manage was a nod because, admittedly, the girl took my damn breath away.

She's pretty, Sera Ventilli. Prettier than I remember every time I see her. I'm almost ashamed to admit that she fills me with a primal need I *know* cannot be quenched by the sweat of anyone else. I didn't expect it to be easy, working for the mob, but with Sera as my sole responsibility, it's going to be harder than I ever imagined.

Outside, she bounces down the stairs, and James, her driver, opens the door of her town car for her. Without a glance over her shoulder, she slips inside, sliding along the leather seats to the far window. Her short dress glides high on her thigh and my gaze slips. I can't help it.

Swallowing hard, I slip right in next to her, earning a big frown from James and an even bigger scowl from Sera.

"No," she says, her perfect lips pouting. "You have your own car."

Her annoyance amuses me. I'm aware it's customary for me to follow her car in one of my own, but I know how this works. The last time she went out, she was able to give her guard the slip. Then, she met me and we were all over each other by ten p.m.

That's not happening tonight. She's not leaving my sight.

"I'd rather ride with you." I turn to James, the mature, white-haired driver, who looks to Sera for approval. "We're fine."

He closes the door and Sera's sweet perfume engulfs me. It dances along my pores, teasing. Taunting. I recall it from the night we spent together and it does things to my blood that it shouldn't.

"Don't get used to this, Ben. You'll lose me tonight and in turn, lose your job."

I smile at her. She seems so certain. "I don't think so, princess."

Sera tosses her bag to the floor and snaps closer

to me. Her firm breasts press against my arm and I try hard to force my thoughts elsewhere. "How'd you find me? Do you think this is a game?"

Her well-shaped eyebrows pull together, her dark eyes flashing dangerously.

"I didn't *find* you. I'm just as shocked as you are."

"Bullshit."

"You've got some fucking nerve to be mad at me, Sera," I point out. "*You* lied to *me*. About your age, about everything."

The driver door opens and Sera reaches across from me, slapping a button to pull up the partition. I hold my breath as her chest touches mine. *She's your job, not your plaything.* I tighten my jaw against the urge to touch my lips to the slope of her neck—which I hate that I know she likes.

"It was supposed to be one night," she retorts, screwing her face up in a way that tightens my stomach. "I don't have to tell a *fling* my whole life story."

"I didn't want your life story. Your correct age would have been nice though."

"You wouldn't have cared anyway. As long as they're getting what they want, men don't care about age."

"I care," I shoot back, louder than necessary, making her flinch. I've always been a law-abiding citizen. I decided on what I believed to be right and wrong a long time ago and I've stuck by it...until *her*. "I bought you alcohol."

"Yeah, you bought me alcohol. A lot of it." She leans close, a sinister quirk on her red lips. "You got me drunk, then you took me back to your hotel room, and you *fucked* me."

I flick my stare to the partition. Is it soundproof? Can he hear? I don't think she'd be saying these things if he could. James rolls the car slowly down the drive and I force my attention back to Sera. Fuck her for trying to put this all on me, like she wasn't a consenting adult the night she grabbed my cock in her hand and pulled me into her greedy, little body.

"If I recall the event correctly, *you* were the one on top fucking *me.*"

Her lips part, my choice of words forcing her to remember the night we shared.

"Doesn't matter how you phrase it. My father is only gonna see it one way." She reaches out with her manicured hands and touches my top button. "You're going to fail tonight, Ben, and you'll tell my father you're not capable of doing the job. He'll let you go, unharmed, I promise…but if you stay…and you drag this out too long, it won't end well for you."

I meet her eyes and, dare I say, they glisten with concern. She wants to keep me safe? What about her? Who's going to keep her safe?

I pull my button out from under her grasp. "I can take care of myself."

Frustration returns to her stare and she's fucking tormenting me with those pouty lips.

"Fine." She huffs, sliding back to her side of the car. "Don't say I didn't warn you."

My blood burns with the challenge. She thinks she's getting away from me tonight, I can see it burning in her pretty eyes, but she's in for a rude awakening.

Sera

When I enter my father's most popular club, Ben is nowhere to be seen. I'd like to think I lost him, but I seriously doubt that's the case. Somehow, I can feel his stare on me. The hair on the back of my neck hasn't settled since the car ride. God, if James wasn't driving, I'd have taken Ben in my mouth right then and there. He has that effect on me. He has this arresting magnetism that completely immobilizes me and...and if my dad ever finds out...Ben is as good as dead.

I try to forget all about Ben when my friends arrive, but I can't. I'd drink to help, but no one is going to serve me at this club. They all know my face. They all know what Marco Ventilli will do to them if they supply his underage daughter with booze.

While my friends drink and have a good time, all I can do is sit and stew on my frustrations.

Until I've had enough.

I snag Naomi by her elbow, spilling a few drops of her drink on her pink halter dress. "Let's go somewhere else."

She tilts her head to the side and her large, gold hoops twirl in the lobes of her ears. "You're not having fun?"

"Do I look like I'm having fun? Everyone else is halfway to wasted and I'm bored out of my brain. I want to go to a different club."

"Okay, let me find the girls and we can go."

I nod. "I'll wait by the bar."

I perch on a cushioned stool by the bar, ignoring the way the bartender gives me uncomfortable side glances, pluck a clean toothpick from its dispenser, and run it in circles against the wood grain surface.

"You look depressed."

Ben's voice is low and coarse, sending a tidal wave of shivers down my spine. I don't realize until I straighten my posture and drop my elbow off the edge of the bar that I was slouching.

"You're supposed to watch from a distance," I point out, continuing to circle the toothpick until the very tip breaks off.

"I was until Naomi bailed on you."

I flick the toothpick over the edge, somewhere, and turn my attention to him. He stands tall beside me, his dark eyes soft and amused, the corner of his mouth slightly turned up.

"She didn't bail on me. We're going someplace else."

Ben's amusement evaporates off his face, replaced by displeased straight eyebrows and lips. "No, you're not."

Across the floor, I see Naomi and Karen, their arms linked together, laughing as they make their way toward us. They haven't spotted us yet and I know Naomi is going to lose her shit if she sees Ben. She's only just stopped asking me about the night we spent together and I'd rather not open that can of worms again—definitely not in my father's club where anyone can hear.

I slip off the stool and my body slides against

his. He doesn't step back and my heart races. I tilt my head on an angle as Ben glares down at me. A dangerous position we've caught ourselves in, but he refuses to move. It seems he isn't as afraid of my family as he should be.

"I'd like to see you physically stop me."

He remains still, searching my face for something. If he's expecting me to stand down, then he's out of his mind. Simpering, I step around him and he clamps his large hand around my forearm and tugs me back. I gasp. None of my father's men have ever touched me. They're too afraid to, but Ben? He touches me like he has every right to.

Dad would kill him.

I pull against him, but he doesn't release me. A couple standing behind Ben murmur and move out of the way, giving us privacy. Do we look like bickering lovers? The thought awakens butterflies in the pit of my belly.

"Why are you so selfish?" he demands, his voice as cold as ice, and I flinch.

Is that how he sees me? Selfish? A spoiled princess? A liar? I imagine I've fallen far from the pedestal he put me on that fateful night. I don't want to upset him or tarnish the long, passionate moment we spent together, but he's left me with no choice. Unless he throws me over his shoulder and carries me home, I'm going to do whatever I want.

"I'm trying to help you, Ben." It takes all of my energy to keep my voice calm.

"I don't need your help." His eyes flick between each of mine and I don't think I've ever seen a pair so fierce, so determined.

And it scares me.

"Ben? Oh, my God." Naomi's shrill excitement sends chills down my spine. "Hey, Sera, look. It's Ben!"

He releases my arm and cold air sweeps in, cooling the fire under my skin.

"Yeah," I deadpan. "It's Ben."

He offers an abrupt and impatient hello, excusing himself before she can ask about Chad.

I glare after him as he effortlessly disappears into the crowd across the room, like he has somewhere to be.

"What's his problem?" Naomi asks, reaching out to tuck a stray lock of hair behind my ear.

"I don't know." I fan my face with my hand, desperate to rid myself of the heat our conversation caused under my skin. "Can we get out of here?"

"I found Karen, but not Hannah."

Karen, my petite brunette friend, wearing heels taller than the Empire State, flicks her long ponytail over her shoulder. "Screw Hannah. She's more interested in finding a new boy toy than hanging out with her friends."

"So, she's not coming?"

They shrug. Ugh. Good enough for me. I push off the bar and head for the exit. The security guards, a.k.a. my father's men in disguise, watch me closely, but none of them stop me because, well, it's not their job.

Outside, James relaxes against the hood of the town car, reading a newspaper under the bright red and white neons. He flicks his attention up for a second, hesitating when he sees me, before stuffing the newspaper under his slender arm.

He clears his throat as he approaches. "Miss Ventilli?"

"Take us to *Beat*, please."

He rushes alongside the car and opens the passenger door. Naomi and Karen throw themselves inside with a rich giggle and I grab the doorframe in my hand.

"And Ben? Will he be riding with you?" James wonders aloud and I pause for the briefest second, glancing over my shoulder.

Ben is nowhere to be seen.

Interesting, considering I told him I was leaving. Did he give up? Did he finally take me at my word? Tonight is his first night on the job. No one expects much from him—not even my father. If Ben fails, he fails. No handsome faces will be beaten, no fingers will be lost. I'm doing this for *him*. He might never see it that way, but I'm not having his death on my conscience.

I lower myself onto the seat.

"Just go, James."

CHAPTER EIGHT

Ben

She thinks she's lost me.

I let her think that.

For some reason, she's pinned me as a weak party boy who can't handle men like her father. I was in the fucking military, for crying out loud, and the things I did during my service...they make me no better than Marco.

I peer out into the streets of Las Vegas, ignoring the stench of vodka and puke in the back of the taxi. I rarely think about what I had to do when I was overseas. It doesn't matter if the life you take is that of your enemy. It affects you all the same. Sometimes, you get caught up in the battle and you do things that prevent sleep later that night and for many nights to come...I shiver at the thought. Anyway, that's not my life anymore, and while I have to live with the hard decisions one has to make in combat, I refuse to let that part of my service define me.

"You haven't given me an address." The taxi driver bites out as he's caught in another red light. "How am I supposed to know what lane to get in?"

"Just follow that town car," I tell him for the umpteenth time. "It'll stop soon. When it does, give it a little breathing space. Pull over only when I tell you to."

"That's awfully cryptic," he mutters, his southern accent coming through. "You're not going to do anything illegal, are ya?"

I chuckle. "Not tonight."

I glance out into the street, the drops from the light spattering of rain has created a bokeh effect on the glass. We're in need of a decent downpour, but the clouds filled with promise have long since gone. They drizzled enough rain to make Vegas look like it's been dipped in glitter, but not enough to make its reckless inhabitants slip and fall on their asses.

I peer between the driver and the passenger seat as Sera's town car slows to a stop and pulls alongside the curb. I instruct my driver to hang back a little and I catch his gaze as he analyzes me through the rearview mirror.

"What'd you say your name was?" he asks.

He doesn't trust me. Good. It's modern America. He shouldn't trust anybody.

"I didn't."

James rushes from the driver seat and I watch intently, ignoring the incessant honks behind me.

"Hey, guy, I can't sit in traffic like this."

I wait a few more seconds as James opens the rear door and the girls pour onto the street, laughing as if they don't have a single care in the world.

Naomi and her friend start forward toward the club's dingy entrance, but Sera takes a second to check her surroundings. She doesn't spot me sitting in the taxi thirteen feet away. Thanks to the shower, the raindrops on the glass reflect the outside world. Nervously flicking her tongue between her lips, she tugs her handbag onto her shoulder and walks toward the entrance of the club, toward the burly, bald-headed bouncer that blocks the door.

I instruct my driver to pull over and he does without hesitation. He asks me for my name again, but I pretend I don't hear him as I fish cash from my wallet and slap it onto the center console. He grabs at it quickly, eager to count the money before I exit the vehicle.

"It's all there," I tell him, watching the girls enter the club. "Plus the tip."

Folding the money, he stuffs it into the front pocket of his red plaid shirt and I slip from the taxi. I barely close the door before he zooms back into traffic without indicating, like a madman.

A vibrating sensation from my cellphone against my left ass cheek demands my attention and I pull it out and answer with a gruff hello.

"You left my club." Marco's voice is cold, so cold I'm surprised ice doesn't seep from the ear piece. "I told you not to leave my club."

"Did you try telling your daughter that?" I retort, storming toward the entrance.

"She doesn't listen," he spits. "Are you with her?"

"I'm not with her," I say, shrugging uncomfortably in my sports jacket. "But I'm near her."

Marco simmers in the silence. Through the phone, I hear him tapping something, apparently in thought. "She's safe?"

"She's safe."

"And you'll bring her home before two?"

I nod even though he can't see me. "She'll be home before two."

Within four feet of the door to the club, I'm stopped by the bouncer, his humongous palm spread, forbidding me from entering.

"What?" I ask him, frowning.

He doesn't say a word. He just shakes his head at me. What the hell? I've never been denied entry to a nightclub before. What is it? Is it the way I'm dressed? I bet it's these damn leather shoes.

"You got a problem, Ben?" Marco asks and his gravelly voice gives me an idea.

"This Neanderthal won't let me inside the club your daughter's at," I tell him. "Obviously, he doesn't think it's important that I get inside."

"Put him on the phone," Marco demands and I hand my cellphone over.

The bouncer hesitates, however, before taking my phone and holding it to his massive, cauliflower ear. He grunts his hello, but his spine straightens the second he gets a response. His eyes widen, his jaw clenching.

God. Having the kind of power Marco does must feel magnificent.

"She paid me…" he grumbles, "…to not let the douche in the sports jacket inside if he shows up. Okay…yes. Okay…all right…"

Douche in the sports jacket? Nice.

The bouncer hands me back my phone and steps aside. I press my phone to my ear.

"If you lose her, Ben Campbell, tonight will not end well for you."

My lips twitch as I fight a smile. "There's no way your girl is getting away from me, Marco. Not tonight."

He hangs up and I slip my phone back into my pocket and enter the nightclub.

Sera

I let my annoyance with Ben consume me for a good hour before I toss the thoughts of him out of my head and swallow my fourth shot of tequila. The bartender knows who I am. He used to work for my father, but he doesn't bring it up. He didn't even card me when I ordered the first round of drinks.

I'm being stupid tonight. Reckless. Dad's gonna kill me when he sees I've been drinking, but I'm over caring and I'm going to need the booze if I'm gonna get through telling him that I ditched Ben hours ago.

Can't wait to see what my punishment is this time. Insert sarcasm here.

"You're not dancing!" Naomi screams in my ear as she falls against the bar.

I laugh at her and her sloppiness. She's never been able to hold her booze well. Who was that guy from weeks ago? Ben's friend? I tap my finger against my empty shot glass and it hits me. Chad. Naomi never boned Chad because she was too busy throwing up. Instead of the revenge fuck she'd been planning since her boyfriend of four years cheated on her, she spent the night half-naked with her arms wrapped around a toilet. Typical Naomi shit.

"I don't want to dance," I shout back, swaying on my seat.

I see her clearly...or at least I think I do. Her red lipstick is smudged and her lips are swollen, the telltale sign of an epic kiss. Or a shitty drunken one.

"You do! You do!" She snatches me by the wrist and tugs me off my stool.

My handbag falls to the ground and I shout at Naomi. "Wait!"

She releases my wrist and I stumble, falling to my knees on the gross club floor. I've long since let my hair out of its bun and it falls around my face, sticking to my damp skin.

Giggling, I grab my handbag and pick myself up. I slam my handbag onto the bar, toward the bartender, the one who used to work for my dad.

"Can you look after this for me?"

He scratches at his short, blond locks and I see the terror in his eyes. He's worried because I'm drunk off my ass and he's the one who's been serving me all night. Lucky for him, no one is here to see. I narrow my eyes at him and he takes my bag with a hesitant nod.

"Good boy."

I turn around and Naomi takes my hand, I let her escort me onto the dancefloor and it's hotter here than it was at the bar. I breathe through my mouth and I taste everything. Deodorant. Booze. Sweat. I'm sure I'd find it gross if I was sober, but right now, it's an airborne drug, inciting arousal deep within me. Naomi presses her hard body against mine as we dance. Her hands roam me, from my hips to my breasts, and I don't mind it. We've touched each other before.

Sexually.

Experimentally.

It was fun, but we decided after the first time that it wasn't something we particularly craved with one another. Unlike my night with Ben...

Hell...I've never felt so good.

I try to imagine Naomi's hands as Ben's, but they're too soft, too feminine. She can't touch me the way he touched me. His hands were powerful and relentless, roaming every naked inch of me.

Soon, Naomi's hands fade from my body and new ones come. Hard ones. *Manly* ones. The stranger grinds against me, his jeans rubbing the back of my bare legs. Whoever he is, he's easier to imagine as Ben. I keep my eyes closed and continue to dance. Not for him, this...this stranger, but for who I imagine this stranger to be. I can count the amount of people I've had sex with on one hand and Ben dominates them all. From what I can remember, and I hope it's not just the drunk haze, he completely claimed me, and in that moment, I'd never felt so pretty, so wanted. That in itself makes our rebellious night worth every risk.

The stranger touches me all over and I allow it, placing my hands over his. I pretend he's someone else, as they travel the length of my body, pinching and squeezing. Arousal builds deep within me for all the wrong reasons, and if I don't sort it out, it will drive me fucking crazy. For a brief second, the stranger's hands fall away, but they come back firmer than ever…and larger than before. I open my eyes to gain clarity of the situation, wondering if there are more than two hands on my body since the large expanse of his palms cover a lot of ground. His hands can easily be mistaken for Ben's. I wonder if his lips can too.

I try to turn around, but he pins me against his torso, his thick arms trapping me against him. That's when I realize that gone is the rough sensation of denim against my legs, replaced by the soothing feel of expensive, Italian wool.

"You're not being cooperative, Seraphina."

I startle, my blood hotwired by the aggression in his tone and then electrified by the use of my full name.

Ben-Goddamn-Campbell.

How long has he been here? Has he watched me all night? Watched me tip back shot after shot? I paid that fucking doorman three hundred dollars to keep him out.

Ben cranes his head, his lips grazing the shell of my ear. The hair on the back of my neck reaches for him, like they're scraps of metal and his lips are magnets. "I was going to let you enjoy your night in peace, but you can't get away with dancing like that. Not with *him*."

He holds me tightly in his grasp and my eyes flutter shut, allowing myself to melt into him. I shouldn't. I normally wouldn't, but he feels so perfect against me. Better than ever. Would he do it? Do me? What if I begged? What if I forced myself on him like I did that night we spent together?

Maybe I shouldn't look at having him as my guard as a bad thing. Maybe it's a good thing. A *very* good thing.

I open my eyes as I succumb to a sudden wave of sobriety.

This is Vegas…

…and my father owns Vegas. If *anyone* who is *anybody* sees us like this, Ben is as good as dead. The whole reason I'm being so difficult, the whole reason I'm keeping him at arm's length is because of that. If I was anyone else's daughter, I'd be chasing him, not pushing him away.

I struggle against him and he lets me go. I whirl on my heel, losing my balance. Cursing, he snatches my wrist and tugs me upright.

I snatch my limb back with a scowl. "Don't touch me."

"Don't touch you?"

"Yeah." I straighten my dress and flick my hair. "You heard me."

"Fine. I'll let you fall on your ass next time."

I narrow my eyes. The neon and the strobes surrounding us flash their colors, the brighter ones lighting his handsome features. When the beat slows, the colors don't flash as much and shadows pool in the hollows of his face, making him look more like one of my father's men than I'd like him to. It strikes me then, as I stare into his soulless eyes, that I don't know a damn thing about him. The fact my father sees something in him should be a warning sign. He doesn't go around hiring good guys, after all.

"I'm going to the bathroom," I shout over my shoulder as I whirl on my heel. "Is that okay, or do you need to hold my hand?"

"Ten minutes. Then we leave."

I mock him, pulling a face as I push my way through the crowd toward the ladies' room. Thankfully, there isn't much of a line and I waltz right in. Five of the seven stalls are unoccupied and I choose the one that's the least gross and I do my business. The bathroom fills up within minutes and soon there are women screeching and laughing, some of them crying uncontrollably. My head spins as I finish my business, push myself to my feet, pull up my panties, and flush the toilet. I sway on my feet. It's slight, but enough for me to feel intimidated by the height of my heels. *Maybe it's time for me to go home.* If I get drunker than this, there's no way I'll be able to hide it from my father. I adjust my dress and fumble with the toilet door latch until it finally opens. I ignore the gaggle of girls as they throw themselves around the room, leaning up against whatever stable sliver of tile and porcelain is free. On the plus side, the bathroom now smells like perfume.

I wash my hands in the basin and dry them with a paper towel before exiting. Outside in the hall, the line of girls begins to stack up. Thank God, I got in when I did.

"Hey." I'm stopped before I can even start forward.

I lift my head to the man in front of me, cringing at his bright red button up shirt he's rolled to the elbows of his slender arms.

"Hello."

Two women cuss at me as they squeeze between me and the door and I shrug it off with a step to the side, intending to bypass the unknown man who's come out of nowhere.

"Sorry." He touches my bicep and I pause. "My name's Jacob. We were dancing together…before your jealous ex showed up."

I quirk an eyebrow, but quickly squash it. A jealous ex? Is that how Ben looked? The thought ignites butterflies in my stomach. As quickly as I can, I take in the man's boyish face and broad shoulders. He's not ugly at least, but he's not the type I'd go for. I like dark eyes, not baby blues.

"Oh." I touch my hair, glancing down the corridor. "Sorry. He can be a little…*intense*."

Where is he, anyway? Surely my father told him to chase away any boys that look me in the eye too long.

"You don't need to apologize." Jacob's purses his thin lips as he scratches at the back of his head. It draws my attention to the copious amounts of gel he's used to slick back his blond locks. "You wanna get out of here? Clear your head a bit?"

I lean back, swaying ever so slightly. I may be under the influence, but I'm not *that* under the influence.

"I'm not sleeping with you, if that's what you think."

He flashes me his palms, a calming gesture, like I'm some wild animal he's worried will flip out. "Furthest thing from my mind, promise. I'm just offering to help give you a little space between you and him. That's all."

I narrow my eyes, suspicious. "That's all, huh?"

"Unless you want to leave with him."

I snort. I can imagine it now, the awkwardness of it all. And he *is* mad at me for dancing with Jacob. You know what? Fuck it. One last ditch effort to save Ben's life.

"Fine, but I'm bringing my friends."

"That's okay with me."

I agree to meet Jacob by his black Mustang in the club's parking lot once I've rounded up Naomi and Karen. Naomi isn't hard to find. She's dancing on a table barefoot with a bottle of booze clenched in her hand and a security guard shouting from three feet away. He can't reach her. She's created a moat of adoring fans around her.

I grab my bag from the bar and use it as a battering ram to get through. I shout her name and she spots me immediately.

"Come on!" she shouts, a glistening liquid rolling from her lips and off her chin. "Dance!"

"I'm leaving!" I shout back. "Are you coming?"

Naomi glances around. "We're thinking about going to a casino soon. You don't want to come?"

I shake my head, aggravating a brewing headache at the back of my skull. I can't have fun here. Ben might have been my acquaintance first, but now my father pays his bills, who knows what information he'll pass on. At least no one is watching me in my room at home. It's the one place I have privacy. The average twenty-year-old American girl would feel suffocated, but I've been dealing with this my whole life. It's just the way it is for girls like me.

I wave Naomi off and she promises to call me when she gets home so I know she arrived safely. It's funny. I've gone out a lot with my friends over the years, but we always end up going our separate ways at some point during the night. Sometimes by accident. Others on purpose. I honestly don't know why I bother going out anymore. I simper. I'm twenty and I'm already sick of the nightlife.

Surprisingly, I don't feel Ben at my back as I make for the club's exit. Since I arrived, the bodies in the club have doubled, maybe even tripled, but I look the same as at least ten other girls in there. I bet Ben the newbie is having a hard time trying to pin me down.

I've never left a club with a guy before, excluding Ben of course, but Jacob is my last shot at getting Ben fired. When I show up at home without James, in the passenger seat of a car driven by a random boy I met at a club my father doesn't own, *and* drunk, there's no way my father will keep Ben on. He might get an ass beating, but he'll recover. At least he won't be found buried under six-feet of sand years down the track and he'll have me to thank for that.

Outside, the air is thick with moisture and it clings to my skin. As I walk along the sidewalk toward the parking lot adjacent the club, I start to doubt my plan. I could be getting myself into a lot of trouble…and not from my dad. I don't know Jacob…I don't know if he's under the influence of alcohol or drugs, and I sure as hell don't know if he has a history of violence or sexual assault. Tonight could end really badly for me.

Granted, leaving the club with Ben that night could have ended badly as well, but there was something about him that made me feel safe. He could have driven me away in a van that had "free candy" sprayed in red up the sides and I still wouldn't have questioned his intentions

While Jacob looks friendly enough, I didn't get that same "safe" vibe and that, suddenly, makes me uncomfortable.

I glance down the main street, looking for James. When he dropped us off, he pulled into a two-minute zone. While my father's men would cut the fingers off any tow truck driver or law enforcement officer that dare lay a finger on their cars, James is different. He's an old man that respects the law and follows the rules. He's been my driver since I was a little girl and my father trusts his driving skills wholeheartedly. Knowing all of this about him, it's safe to say he's parked the town car elsewhere. Pausing, I open my handbag and pull out my new phone. Sure enough, James has texted to let me know he's parked around the back when I'm ready to leave. I'm thankful my father only depends on James to drive me around and not to protect me. I can't stomach the thought of James getting into trouble because of something I did.

I turn into the alley, eager to find James instead of Jacob as second guesses plague me.

To my left, a car door clicks open. "Hey!"

I slam to a stop and squint through the murky, yellow streetlight at the red-draped arm that waves in my direction.

"Over here!"

Shit.

"Where are your friends at?"

"They don't want to come," I shout back, glancing around, scratching the back of my head. "I think I'm gonna call it a night and go home."

"Okay." Jacob smiles. "Want me to take you home?"

Cold feet. That's what they call the act of backing out of something at the last minute. My feet aren't just cold. My feet are freezing. If Ben wants to work for my family, that's fine. Whatever happens is on him. I shouldn't risk my safety trying to protect him.

"Um…"

"She's good."

I startle at the rough snap beside me as Ben storms down the sidewalk. I take a minute step back as he swallows the distance between us, looking as devastating as ever.

"You sure?"

I cringe at Jacob's question, realizing I don't know Ben's temperament either. He could be a madman. I swiftly nod, unable to take my eyes off Ben, who glares down his straight nose at me, and I swallow hard.

"Ben is going to take me home."

Ben's jaw ticks and my body weakens as his arresting aggression rolls off of him in waves. I've really made him angry tonight. The way he's poised his eyebrows, with a challenging kink in their curve, suggests he's reached the end of his rope.

Jacob curses and drops back into his car. The black Mustang comes to life with a roar and I jump as he floors it out, racing off like an idiot. Jacob's tires screech in the distance, followed by the various honks of other drivers, and I'm thankful Ben showed up in time to stop me from being polite and getting in Jacob's car, even though I didn't want to.

"Ben…"

"You know where James has parked. I suggest you start walking before I say something I'll regret."

Okay…fair enough. Pursing my lips, I turn around, slipping my cellphone into my handbag. My heels click along the pavement and I desperately try to keep my focus on each crack as I pass them by, not wanting to lose a shoe or roll my ankle. The more I focus on my feet, however, the more I notice a niggling at the back of my heel. Soon, that niggling turns into full blown fire. I stop with a groan.

"My feet hurt."

He nudges my shoulder. "It's not far, princess."

Princess? I whirl around to face him. "Stop calling me that."

"I will, when you stop acting like one."

Tears well in my eyes—irrational tears. Ones born of alcohol and pain. He can say what he wants about me. It isn't wrong. I've been horrible since I saw him having breakfast with my father in my backyard.

"I…" I clear my throat. "I think I have a blister."

The longer I stay in these shoes, the more I notice the pain. I swipe at my cheek and peer up at

Ben, who watches me closely, his head tilted, his eyebrows furrowed. He doesn't trust me.

"You want me to carry you?"

I scoff with a sniffle. "In this dress? No."

"Then what do you want?" His voice holds an air of impatience and I don't like it.

I was going to ask him to take my shoes off, but he'll only mock me for that too. Tsking, I bend over and my handbag slides down my arm and plonks to the ground, pulling me off balance.

I put my hand out and squeeze my eyes shut, bracing for impact, but it doesn't come.

"Christ," Ben curses, grabbing my arm in one hand while smoothing a large, rough palm over the small of my back. He eases me upright and my head spins, my eyes fluttering open.

I grin at him. "I thought you were going to let me fall on my ass next time."

"I thought about it."

I touch his bicep to steady myself and I realize he's taken off his sports jacket. Only thin, silky fabric separates my warm, damp skin from his. I try not to let it bother me, but there's something about that thought that gets me hot underneath my metaphorical collar.

"Hold onto this for me." Releasing me, he drapes his sports jacket over my shoulders and I turn my head into the fabric to smell it, leaning against the club's concrete wall behind me.

It smells like him…like he did the night we spent together. Earth. Man. A perfect mix of sugar and spice.

Not paying me any attention, Ben crouches

before me, placing one gentle hand on the back of my calf and the other on my heel. I become hyperaware of his bare skin on mine and goosebumps erupt along the narrow of my spine.

"Lift," he orders and I do as I'm told.

Cool air swoops in and kisses my aching feet, and I can't help the melting sigh that seeps from my lips. I place my tender sole against the uneven concrete and snuggle further into his sports jacket as he removes my second heel and straightens his stance.

"Better?"

I nod without a smile. "Much. Thank you."

I push off the wall and stroll the rest of the alley, moving at a snail's pace so I don't end up with a new shoe, one made of syringes and shards of broken glass. I exhale in relief when I spot my town car by the club's rear entry and James's silhouette inside. As usual, he jumps out as I approach, but Ben waves him off. "I've got it, James. Thanks."

James returns to the driver's seat and Ben opens the door for me. I slip inside and shuffle along the leather seats to the far door, placing my handbag on my lap. Once Ben joins me, he slams the door shut and raises the partition between us and James, placing my heels neatly in the space beside him.

With my head against the window, I sit in silence for what feels like years, zoning in and out of stupors, and after a while, it gets to me.

"I know you're mad at me..." I start, lifting my forehead off the glass.

"That's the understatement of the fucking century."

"But I was only going to leave with him to help you."

He turns in his seat, settling his dark gaze on me. "Help me? If you want to help me, why don't you stop making my job so damn difficult?"

I open my mouth to reply, but he cuts me off.

"You think I want to follow you around town and stand in the corner of some nightclub while you drink your ass off and dance on strangers? I fucking don't, but I am committed to seeing this job through because I get to carry a loaded gun and your father pays me more than I ever made in the army." He turns his large body to face the front of the car. "This job isn't about you. I need it because I can't go back to bagging groceries or fetching coffee. I can't do mediocrity."

I pull his jacket tighter around me. I didn't know he was in the army…

"You can play your games as much as you want, Sera, but you cannot get rid of me." His dark, gravelly tone makes me shiver. "I'll be there, right behind you, until your father buries a bullet in my skull."

I peer at him. "And that doesn't scare you?"

"What?"

"My father…when he finds out what we did?"

Ben's jaw flexes as he ponders, and the longer he holds me in his thoughtful gaze, the faster my heart beats.

"No."

"He'll kill you."

"Maybe, but that won't erase what we did."

I tap my manicured fingers against my knees,

watching as the bright colors of Vegas reflect in the clear acrylic.

"Do you regret what we did?" A stupid question, but I ask it anyway.

We were both wasted that night. I don't remember all of it, but the snippets I do still set my blood on fire. Ben Campbell knows his way around a woman, that's obvious. He's had a hundred women, probably. I bet I barely made a blip on his radar.

When he doesn't answer, I muster the courage to look at him. He's watching me, one hand closed tightly around the handle to the arm rest.

"Do you?" he counters and, dare I say, his voice is almost sad.

I open my mouth and the words I was going to say become trapped in my throat as James lowers the partition. "We're going home, right, Miss?"

"Yes, thank you, James."

With an impatient sigh, Ben mutters under his breath and closes the partition.

"I guess neither of us remembers enough of that night to truly form an opinion."

"Speak for yourself."

I cut my eyes at him. "You drank as much as I did."

Ben's full lips twitch at the corners and he fights one of those smiles I like so much. "I'm curious to hear how *you* think the night panned out since you're already wrong."

"Wrong?" I turn on the seat, facing him front on.

"Yeah, wrong. You outdrank me a hundred to one."

I frown. "No, I didn't."

"Whatever helps you sleep at night."

"That's not how I remember it," I argue. "Next you're going to tell me that I threw myself at you? That going back to Chad's suite was *my* idea?"

Ben leans close, his eyes glistening with delight. "Yes, you *did* throw yourself at me. No, it wasn't your idea to go back to Chad's suite."

I settle against the leather seat, smug.

"If I let you have it your way, you would've fucked me in the corner booth of a random Vegas club instead of every surface in a two grand a night hotel room."

I gape at him. Fierce heat rushes into my cheeks and blooms all over my body. Where does he get the nerve to talk to me like that? Like I'm some kind of…of…*whore.*

"That's not how it happened." I shrug out of his jacket and toss it to the floor along with my bag.

Is it hot in here? I hit the partition button and request James cool the air before closing him off once again. Ben's cockiness radiates off of him in waves and it irritates the hell out of me. How dare he sit there all unbothered. Who the hell does he think he is?

"Can't take the heat, princess?"

"I've already asked you not to call me that."

He shrugs his big, broad shoulders and lifts my heels in front of his face. "If the shoes fit."

Clenching my teeth, I launch at him, knocking my shoes to the floor. He barely flinches, barely reacts to my outburst. As I pant in anger next to him, all he does is look at me, his chin slightly tilted toward his chest, his darkening stare penetrating my soul from under his brow.

"You're wild…" he says in a low deep voice. "Aren't you?"

"I'm anything, but a princess."

James rolls to a stop at a red light and bright, white LEDs infiltrate the black, bulletproof glass, illuminating Ben's features. His spiky black hair, dark eyes that—in this moment—threaten to share all of his deepest, darkest secrets with me.

…and don't get me started on those full lips of his.

Lips I want to kiss.

Ben flicks his tongue over his lower lip to moisten it and it pulls me out of my daze.

We're close, I realize. So close I can smell him—feel his warmth radiating onto me, urging me to reach out and touch him.

"You don't remember anything about that night?"

I give my head a lazy shake.

"Not how I kissed you?"

I close my eyes and desperately try to remember. I bet it was fucking glorious. "No."

"Not how I touched you?"

I feel his hot breath on my face and my pulse skitters uncontrollably. I don't dare open my eyes. The thought of having him so close…my heart can't take it.

"Look at me…" he utters and I force my eyes to flutter open. "I'll refresh your memory if you promise not to *ever* run off on me again."

Is…is he negotiating with me? A kiss in

exchange for my compliance?

"You think your kiss is worth it, huh?"

My amused tone makes his eyes glisten with a challenge and he smiles, one corner of his mouth turning up, as he rolls the sleeves of his white button shirt to his elbows.

"Are all soldiers as dramatic as you?"

He chuckles. "Only when their dignity is on the line."

Ben shuffles toward me and I fall back against the leather with a nervous laugh. "Ben, this is stupid."

"No, it isn't."

He leans closer and fire burns in my cheeks. He's serious. He really wants to do this.

"James…" I whisper, my attention falling to Ben's lips as he moistens them. "What if he—"

"Don't worry about him."

He glides one rough hand along my outer thigh and gently guides my chin with the other. He lifts my face to his and touches his lips to mine. His kiss is gentle, barely a touch, but it threatens to consume me all the same. My eyes flutter shut and my heart races, threatening to tear a hole in my chest.

This is dangerous.

With a groan, he clamps his hand on my thigh and I gasp as he tugs me forward, pulling me into his lap. The thin fabric around my thighs gives away with smalls pops of threading and I try to assess the damage, but he snatches my face in his large hands, forcing my mouth to remain on his. Ben kisses me hard, so hard he sucks the air from my lungs and the sense from my head. The warmth from my blush spreads down my neck and pools in my breasts. His hands return to gripping my thighs and they're so strong and powerful. I want to feel them over my entire body.

I remember now. This is exactly how I felt that night.

Ben flicks his tongue over my lower lip, coaxing me into opening my mouth to him.

Then he claims it.

He claims it like it's his and *only* his.

Like he's the only one who's ever kissed me.

I moan against him, raking ten aggressive fingers through his clean hair. I open my thighs wider, eager for our hips to touch. His thighs are monstrous, warm, and firm. I moan again, louder this time, and it's enough to break this kiss. I tilt my head back.

"Shut up," Ben growls, pressing his lips to my throat. I swallow hard and he licks my flesh as it bobs. "We'll get caught."

"I don't care," I sigh. "Just keep going."

I tilt my face, meeting his lips once again, this time with wild abandon.

This kiss is worth risking everything for.

This kiss is worth getting murdered for.

I want him. I want him now. In this moment, as wrapped up as I am, I can see myself throwing caution to the wind and taking him anywhere—and any way—I can get him.

I press my breasts against his chest, desperate to get closer. A few wild heartbeats pass and I feel Ben begin to close off underneath me, trying to end the kiss, but I don't want to stop.

I groan in protest and continue to touch him, to kiss him, but he pulls my hands from his body and pins my arms to my side before raking his teeth over my lower lip, ending the kiss.

Disappointment and frustration flood me and I cut my eyes at him. "That wasn't anything to brag about."

My voice is breathless and I hate it. My lips are swollen too, they feel like tiny balloons on my face. Smirking, he eases me off of his lap and the burning skin of my thighs cool against the leather seat.

"If you say so." He bends down and grabs my heels. With a gentle flick of his wrists, he tosses them in front of me. "We're home."

I sit up straight. We're home? Jesus Christ. How long did we kiss for?

"What's the matter?" he asks, his voice teasing as he reaches over and plucks his jacket off the floor. "Lose track of time?"

"No." I slip my bare feet back into my heels, cringing when the leather presses against forming blisters. "Don't be ridiculous. It was a kiss. Not an LSD trip."

Oh, you little liar. Kissing Ben was *more* than any synthetic fantasy I've ever been on. I'm just too stubborn to admit it. Whatever this man has in his saliva needs to be extracted, synthesized, and turned into a drug. No one human should possess the ability to kiss like that.

The car rolls to a stop just as we finish adjusting ourselves. I flick my hair around my shoulders to hide the pink hue of arousal in my skin. I work on evening my breathing when Ben reaches up to the ceiling and turns the light on. I flinch away from it, like a vampire to sunlight.

"What are you doing?"

"You left a wet patch on my pants."

My stomach revolts and I gape at him, mortified. Why is he looking at me like that? As if he's just revealed the punchline to a joke.

"No, I didn't."

He snatches my hand and presses my palm against his warm, damp crotch. My fingers twitch, so does his cock, and his hot breath blows against my cheek. "That's all you."

I snap my hand back with a scoff, feigning disgust to mask the sexual heat that climbs the back of my neck. Reaching up, I turn off the roof light, drowning us in semi-darkness. "You're ridiculous."

"And you're a shitty actress."

James's shadow appears against the passenger's glass a second before he opens Ben's door. I purse my lips, deprived of getting the final say.

Fucking Ben Campbell.

CHAPTER NINE

Ben

She's a piece of work, this girl, but fucking hell, is she beautiful. I stand beside James as Sera climbs out of the car with all the grace in the world. You can't tell she's drank more than she probably should have. You can't tell she spent a good chunk of her night grinding her perfect ass against a stranger. You definitely can't tell she just had the life kissed out of her, not unless you count the small smear of red lipstick to the right of her lips.

"Enjoy the rest of your night, Miss Sera." He looks at me. "Ben."

She smiles sweetly at James. Why can't I get one of those smiles? All I get are sneers and glares.

"Goodnight, James." Sera and I speak in unison and her husky tone meshes wonderfully with mine, but I knew that already.

"If you need to go anywhere now until tomorrow morning, I'm sure Ben will take you."

Fat chance. I'm tired. There's only one place

Sera is going and that's bed.

She marches in front of me and storms the front steps of her house. Inside, all of the lights are still on. I glance at my watch. Midnight. When do these people sleep?

I follow Sera through the house and into the kitchen where her father waits, cutting into a loaf of bread with a knife much too big for the job. His stare flicks over Sera as she dumps her handbag on the counter with a heavy exhale, and opens the ridiculously large fridge for a bottle of orange juice.

"Want a glass, Ben?"

I approach the counter. "Sure."

"Dad?"

Marco shakes his head. "Your dress is torn at the hem."

Sera plays dumb and she does it well. Maybe the girl isn't such a bad actress. "Hm?"

"Your dress." He points to her thigh. "It's torn."

She shrugs her slender shoulders, dipping low into a cupboard for some glass cups. "I danced. Must've happened then."

"What kind of dancing?"

Snorting, Sera tucks hair behind her ear and pours O.J. into the cups. "Normal dancing."

Marco watches her closely as he continues to cut bread with his large knife, wearing a black polo that makes the crumbs on it stand out, like dandruff.

She returns the orange juice to the fridge, grabs her handbag, her cup, and waves her father off before retiring for the night. When she's out of sight, Marco turns his black, soulless stare on me.

"I'm impressed you brought her back before

curfew—without her annoying friends too."

I shrug. "I'm sure she's not happy about it."

"Doesn't matter. Vegas is no place for a girl after midnight." He pinches a large crumb of bread and puts it between his lips. "You got kids?"

I grimace. Is he asking because I look old enough to have children? Perhaps to him, I look old enough to have children around Sera's age. The thought turns my stomach and I shake my head as I grab my glass of orange juice.

"Why give her a two a.m. curfew if you don't want her out so late?" I ask, eager to change the conversation.

"It was her mother's idea. She thinks I'm too strict with Seraphina, but she's naïve. She doesn't know Vegas like I do."

I sip my juice and put it down. "I don't think handling your daughter will be a problem for me."

He nods, dropping the knife. "Good. Listen." He rounds the counter and I try not to look at his gray sweatpants as his chubby body comes into view. "We're having an event here tomorrow evening. This place will be swarming with unsavory characters. I'll have my men here, but I want a set of eyes *only* on Sera. Understand?"

I nod. "Okay."

"Some of the men coming are slimeballs who've had an eye for my daughter since she was young."

I frown. "And you allow them into your house?"

"I don't fucking allow anything when it comes to my little girl," he snaps. "But despite the business, I can't go around slaughtering important people. You get what I'm saying?"

I nod. "So, I keep an eye on her. No problem."

"No." He jabs me in the chest with his index finger. "You keep *two* eyes on her."

I swallow. *Obviously, that's what I meant.*

Marco pushes past me. "All of your shit is in the guest house. I suggest you rest."

I stand in the kitchen, staring into my orange juice. All of my shit is in the guest house? Talk about invasive. Luckily, I'm a minimalist and I don't own much in my little apartment on Vegas's west side. Most of my expensive and sentimental belongings are stored at my mother's house.

I place my glass of orange juice down on the counter and make my way out of the kitchen and into the wide-open backyard. The only sounds to be heard come from the fountain in the pool and a set of sprinklers along the far-right fence.

I shrug out of my jacket and unbutton my shirt. The manor and its grounds have a different feel at night. It's less threatening, less daunting, when it's not littered with criminals standing around waiting for a call. It's serene. A true resting place.

I tug on the front door of the guest house and slip inside. A few handfuls of medium sized boxes litter the vast sitting space. Inside them holds nothing of extreme importance or sentimental value…my uniform, medals, and weapons being the exception. I'm almost too ashamed to look at them now.

The glow through the front windows and door fades as the lights of the house are turned off. Working only with the glow of the moon, I cross the sitting room to a lamp by a bookshelf and I fumble with it until it flicks on, almost blinding me.

I shrug out of my shirt and toss it to the floor. From where I stand, I see the sitting room and a kitchen. Branching off from those is a small hallway that I can only assume leads to the bedroom. My exhaustion draws me to the hallway like a moth to a flame, and I don't fight it. I let it guide me, moving on auto-pilot, until I'm face down on one of the firmest mattresses I've ever laid on. Which is perfect. Most beds are too soft. Unless I'm wasted, I can only sleep on the floor.

I groan, pushing my hands under the pillows to feel the cool fabric as I kick my shoes off. One hits the floor and one doesn't, but I'm dead to the world before I can even think about investigating.

***

I've never been much of a dreamer, but I've dreamt of Sera and the night we spent together on and off since it happened. It's nothing to write home about. We kiss, we touch, we fuck, and I wake up with a raging boner. That's the usual sequence…

…but tonight is different.

Tonight my subconscious clashes with my reality in the strangest of ways. I attempt to open my eyes, but I'm sucked back into dreamland by the most vivid dream I've ever experienced.

Pleasure rolls over my body in powerful waves and all I can see behind my lids are her full glossy lips against my shaft, tracing the vein that runs along the back with her wet, warm tongue.

Reality swiftly interrupts and I shudder, wanting to clench the sheets beneath me in my fists as a groan—my groan—vibrates my chest. But I can't move. My body is still paralyzed from sleep.

Whatever is happening, whatever my brain, my hormones, and that fucking girl is doing to me, I don't want it to stop. I don't want to wake up from this.

Warmth flows from between my legs and my eyes finally flutter open. The wonderful sensation draws me from my sleep, forcing me to feel everything—in *real* time.

I clench the bed sheets and flex my hips until I'm stopped by the back of a throat. I moan, loudly, and a gentle gag noise pulls me from whatever fragments of sleep remain.

I pause—I fucking *freeze*—as the sleep-induced haze begins to wear off. There's no mistaking it. I shudder against the urge to spill my come. There's a very warm, very wet mouth on my cock.

She sucks the tip between her lips while squeezing the thick shaft in her small hands.

"Shit." I squeeze my eyes shut. This is happening…it shouldn't be, but it is. She works me over flawlessly, the perfect combination of slow and fast. Slick, but not sloppy enough to mask the friction of her skin on mine. "Sera?"

I spread my palms against the cool sheets and crane my neck, peering down my naked torso. It's dark, so dark I can't see her face, but I know those lips. I could pick them out of a Goddamn line up. My black slacks are open, the underside of the base of my cock rubs where the zipper's teeth meet at the bottom. How'd she get my pants open without waking me up? I'm the lightest sleeper I know—or *was.* It's a title I'll have to revisit after this.

"Stop," I pant, dropping my head back against the mattress.

I beg her again, but it's pathetic. A rush of air that only increases her assault as she takes me into her mouth and goes deep, until my cock squeezes into her throat. She gags, I clench, crunching my body to place a hand on her head.

"Fucking stop," I grind out between my clenched teeth, but my hand betrays me.

I push and pull her head, coaxing her to keep going deep, until I feel her saliva roll down my shaft and onto my balls. I should stop her. I mean, did she not see the size of the knife her father used to cut bread tonight? I'm willing to bet it's not the biggest—or the sharpest—he owns.

But it just feels…so…damn…good. I'm so close to—*no.*

I grab a fistful of her hair and pull her off my cock with a 'pop.'

"I said stop."

She takes a large gasp of air before diving on me, straddling my waist. I feel it immediately, the wetness on my skin, the warmth radiating from between her legs. "You want me to stop?"

"We can't do this."

I release her hair and she snatches my wrists, pinning them beside my head. My chest rises and falls faster than I want it to and she simpers at the sight.

"You don't want it?" she whispers, brushing her lips against mine. "You don't want me?"

I become hyperaware of my surroundings,

straining my ears to hear the slightest sound of someone's approach.

"What if someone saw you come in? What if they check the surveillance?"

"Don't you worry your pretty little head." She kisses the corner of my mouth, softly biting my bottom lip. "This has been my prison since I was little. I know it like the back of my hand. No one will catch us."

I try to protest again, but it ends on her lips as she slides her tongue into my mouth, overpowering me in the strangest of ways. I've never seen myself as a weak man. In my military career, I've undergone various interrogation simulations and haven't failed a single one. Not when I was starving, not when I was in pain, not even when I was freezing my ass off, the tips of my hair frozen into sharp spurs of ice, but here I am, caving to the pressure of a tiny woman who wants nothing more than to fuck me into oblivion. My superiors would be disappointed.

"If I let go of your wrists, do you promise to touch me?" she whispers against my lips. "Just one more time, Ben. I want to remember it. All of it."

"And afterwards? When I make you come so hard no one else could possibly measure up? I can't have you staring at me from across the room like a lost puppy. Not in front of your father."

"I'm appalled you think a simple fling has the power to make me so obsessed with you and your—"

"You snuck into my bed, at risk of us both getting murdered, just to put my cock in your

107

mouth. Who's to say you're not already obsessed?"

Straightening her spine, she releases my wrists. Her long, black hair curls around her covered breasts and she glares down at me. "I can leave anytime I want."

My lips twitch at the threatening tone in her voice. I've never been one to back down from a challenge.

"So leave."

She remains still, and I know she's analyzing me as best she can in the dark. I hear her lips part with a sigh and she lifts her hips off of me, muttering under her breath as she swings her legs over and turns her back to me. "Suit yourself."

I contemplate letting her go, but my cock throbs painfully. I can't fix this kind of pressure with my hand. It'd take days and countless bottles of lube before it settles.

Sera barely makes it to the edge of the bed when I snatch her by the waist and pin her face down on the bed. Air leaves her lungs, her hands fisting the blankets as I pull her hips up and she holds herself there on her knees. Whatever she was wearing, her white nighty, bunches at her ribs, exposing her complete lower half to me. A tight, wet pussy and an even tighter asshole.

"You can't leave me like this," I tell her, shoving my pants down my thighs. Grabbing my cock, I rub it against her inner thigh and she shivers. "You expect me to walk around with this tomorrow? In front of everyone?"

"That sounds like a Ben problem," she says on exhale. "I'd love to help, but I'm leaving."

I smooth my palm over her ass, relishing in the way it moves and jiggles. "Doesn't look like you're going anywhere."

"I can leave any time I want."

I withdraw my palm a few inches from her flesh before letting it loose and slapping her hard.

She helps, flexing her hips away from me. "Fuck, Ben. What was that for?"

"Maybe you'd listen to me better if I slapped you around a little bit." With my free hand, I touch the slit of her pussy. It's wet, so fucking wet, and pulsating. "Holy shit. That turns you on?"

"No."

I simper. Even she doesn't sound convinced. I slap her ass again and she hisses, curving her spine more, making her pussy open up to me.

I'm weak at the sight, faint but noticeable in the darkness. All of a sudden my mouth is parched, my lips dry with urge to moisten them in her perfect pussy. Shuffling back, I hunch and press my mouth to her opening. She bucks against me, spreading her legs wider, giving me access to everything I want.

I lick her over and over, sucking all of her between my lips. She tastes better than I remember, better than I could ever imagine.

"I don't want to come like this," Sera pants, her legs quivering as she fights an orgasm. "I wanna come like I did that first night. On you. With you."

I pull back, squeezing her ass in my hand. "I thought you didn't remember anything?"

"I remember that."

I pause for the briefest moment, listening for any other sound besides our labored

109

breathing…nothing. Normally, I'd start with some kissing, an hour of nice foreplay, and then dive into the fucking, but I don't have a second to waste here.

I grab my cock at the base of my shaft and press it against her opening, making her breath hitch in her throat.

Fuck. "I don't have a condom."

She presses back on me and her lips surround the head of my cock, begging me to push inside her. "Just pull out."

Pull out? I've never risked it…but shit. I'm too wound up not to try, at least.

For no reason at all, the guy from earlier tonight pops into my head…and the way he touched her. The way she let him touch her…

I drop my body against her, flattening her against the mattress, and grab a fistful of her hair. "How many guys do you leave a club with on a regular basis?"

"What?"

I tighten my grip. "You heard me."

"That question doesn't make me feel like a whore at all." Sarcasm drips from her tone.

"That's not what I was implying."

"That's exactly what you were implying."

I plant a gentle kiss on her temple, to let her know I'm not judging. "How many?"

"Zero." She gasps against the blankets. "You're the only one."

"The only one?"

"Yes…yes, I promise."

Shifting my legs, I push her thighs open and align my cock with her pussy. This is how I'll fuck her first. She's completely dominated by me and it leaves out any possibility of developing a romantic connection.

When we first had sex together, she was on me, her chest to mine, her nose and forehead sliding against my own. In that moment, it was easy to pretend it wasn't a fling, that our session had meaning.

This time it can't have meaning. I can't give it meaning if I want to keep my head on my shoulders where it belongs.

In one swift thrust, I push my cock inside her body and she moans, loudly, just about making me come on the spot. I shush her and she tries her hardest to bite back her pleasure, but the more I move, the more I massage her from the inside, the more reckless she becomes.

"More," she begs, her voice a husky whisper. "More, Ben, more."

I give her more. I give her as much as I can from this position, but her bubbly little ass prevents me from getting all of my cock inside her.

Cursing, I pull out of her and lift my body up on my arms.

"Turn over."

Sera rolls over underneath me, her eyes locking with mine, as I lower myself against her body once more. Her warm, uneven breath blows along my face and she wraps her legs around my waist.

I line myself up and push into her body with a deep groan, burying myself to the hilt, making her breathless.

"I want to come," she whispers, touching my

face.

She traces her soft fingers along my jaw, gently guiding my face to hers. I slow my hips as our lips meet and she slides her tongue into my mouth. I don't pull away. I allow it, allow myself to take part in a kiss that shouldn't be shared between two people like us.

Not while I'm inside her like this.

Sera

My thigh muscles burn as they stretch to accommodate his large body between them. I shouldn't be here, not with him, and at my home of all places. I've always been reckless and rebellious, always, but this is over the top, even for me.

When I went back to my room, I showered and I climbed into bed. I tried reading for a little while, but not even the great Nora Roberts could hold my attention. As I skimmed through pages, pretending to read, I took a call from Naomi, who arrived safely at some random guy's pad.

From there, as I stewed on her carefree social and sex life, I couldn't stop thinking about Ben and our kiss in the car. He made my entire body come to life. How can a young woman like me, twenty and stupid, not obsess over it? Over him?

I went downstairs to see him only for answers about the kiss, but when I saw him lying on his bed, shirtless, his wide, muscular back exposed to me, I couldn't turn away.

He rolled over the moment I approached the bed and my gaze flew to his taught and toned stomach.

The sight of a man in such peak condition had me forgetting why I'd come to see him, but it was the tent in his pants that was my undoing.

Ben breaks the kiss with a groan, pulling me from my thoughts. "You feel so damn good."

He lifts his hips until his cock is completely out of me. I exhale, disappointed at how empty I feel without him inside me. Reaching between us, he grazes the head of his dick against my clit. It slides so effortlessly, stirring my arousal to new heights. "Do you like how that feels?"

"I love it," I breathe. "I love you inside me more."

He kisses me quickly on the lips and I feel his smirk right before he thrusts his hips forward, filling me once again.

"Oh God!"

Rearing back, he pushes my bunched nighty over my tits, exposing them as they bounce with every thrust. "Your tits are going to make me come," he groans. "Grab 'em for me, fucking play with them like I asked you to that night in the hotel "

I do as I'm told and I grab as much of my breasts as I can in my small hands. Ben hunches over me, gripping my hair and bringing his mouth to mine.

"Lick them," he demands, "lick those tits."

I push my breasts together and I lick them, driving Ben wild. Craning his neck, he licks them too, our tongues grazing and I taste my arousal on him.

"I'm trying so hard not to fill your pussy." Tightening his grip in my hair, he fucks me harder. "Fuck, I want to so bad."

I shake my head. "Don't."

"Sera…"

I drop my breasts and I curl my fingers into the cool sheets beneath us as he plunges in and out of me, his movements never wavering from rough and fast. I moan, arching against him, begging him not to stop. Slick sweat begins to form between our bodies as he struggles to hold his weight off of me, eager to get himself deeper and deeper inside.

Ben grabs one of my ankles from behind his back and lifts himself off of me, allowing enough room to wedge my knee against my chest. I clench his shoulders, digging my nails in, as he reaches a new depth, the kind of depth that makes my pussy swell. He alternates his fast, deep strokes for shallow, fast ones and I crunch my body, repeating his name over and over, gasping for air that seems to escape me. It builds up, my orgasm. Like dropped Coke that rushes up the neck of a bottle, it pours out, seizing my entire body.

Ben kisses me, swallowing all of my moans and whimpers. Somehow, I free my leg at the last minute and wrap it tightly around Ben's waist. He jerks back, but I pull him in close and he releases a guttural sound that overpowers my own.

I feel it then, as my daze begins to wear off. My insides pulsate over and over, squeezing him as his does the same…pumping every last drop of him inside of me.

Shit.

CHAPTER TEN

Ben

The next morning

Yeah, I'm fucking nervous.

I'm fucking nervous because last night, Sera broke into my home and seduced me out of an innocent sleep. I'm nervous because she insisted I fuck her without protection and then tightened her grip on me when I tried to pull out.

She lost her shit at me because I came in her, like I'm the one at fault. Me!

I pace the backyard, sticking along the far-right fence line, watching her as she stands beside her mother in a pretty, yellow dress, engaged in conversation with a fat fuck I don't like the look of. With a laugh I *know* is fake, she flicks her long, dark locks over her shoulder and smiles widely, exposing perfect, straight white teeth.

"You look nervous."

I startle, ceasing to pace, and turn to face one of

115

Marco's main men. What'd he say his name was again? Roman, I think. He narrows his black eyes at me and drags on his cigarette, the cherry on the end flaring.

"Do I?"

"Yeah. You're pacing." He exhales, blowing smoke into my face. "I fucking hate it."

My eyebrows pull in. "Oh, yeah? Then go smoke somewhere else."

"Nah, I like it here."

"Suit yourself." I walk away from him, moving along the back of the party, my hands stuffed into my slacks.

There's a lot of people here today, more than I was expecting. According to Marco, this crew is the Giavanni clan, a rival family here in Vegas. At any moment, something could ignite between them. For now, however, things seem cordial. Marco and Ivan Giavanni are inside discussing business about casinos and land while the rest of their people mingle outside.

It feels strange, standing and watching without the heavy weight of a rifle in my hand, but I keep myself busy, fidgeting with a toothpick in my pocket instead. I scan the crowd every few minutes, especially those closest to Sera. Like her father said, she is my only priority here today. Her mother has made my job easy by remaining at her side—until *now,* that is.

The moment her mother leaves, the fat guy with the graying hair moves closer to Sera, whispering in her ear. Sera's gaze flicks to me and my jaw tightens.

I'm not jealous, but if he doesn't watch himself…

"Ooh, you don't like that, do you?"

I snap away from Roman, who has followed me across the yard. "What the hell is your problem?"

"You're my problem. I don't like you."

I smooth the palms of my hands down my black jacket. "Really? Because I'm getting a different vibe."

Roman snickers, dropping his cigarette to the ground and stomping it out with his leather shoe. "Your job is to watch Sera. My job is to watch you."

"Watch me?" I snort. "What for?"

Roman shrugs his broad shoulders. "You know who that is?" he asks, flicking his bald head toward Sera and the man whispering in her ear.

"No clue."

"That's Deena. Ivan's brother and right-hand man. Sad fucker wants to marry the girl."

"Who? Sera?"

Roman nods. "Been begging for her hand since she was a kid."

I grimace. Here I am judging myself harshly for sleeping with a legal and consenting twenty-year-old when there are men who've looked at her sexually before she even went through puberty. It's sickening, and the fact Marco allows them into his home makes him no better. I would burn bridges with all my business partners if any of them expressed interest in my daughter. Hell, I wouldn't just burn bridges. I'd topple skyscrapers and destroy airports.

I knew there was something I didn't like about this Deena guy. "What a vile piece of shit."

"Maybe, but he knows he's in with a chance now."

I cut my eyes at him. "What do you mean?"

"Marco has tried to keep Sera pure, to give her as a gift to another family to strengthen ties through marriage, but the little slut prefers to run around town with her friends, taking cock from God knows who."

Rage coils in my stomach, but I manage to keep it in check. I inhale through my nose, filling my lungs with fresh air while counting to ten. I wonder how Marco would feel, hearing one of his trusted men bad mouth his daughter like that? I mean, a slut? Hardly.

It takes all of my strength not to comment. Mostly because there's only a string of cuss words waiting at the peak of my throat.

"She's getting old, though. Soon Marco is gonna have no choice but to marry her off to one of these gross bastards just to keep some land." He kisses his teeth. "It's a shame really…to see a beautiful body like that be wasted under one like *his.*"

The thought turns my stomach. When Deena pulls back, Sera smiles politely and attempts to step around him, only he snatches her arm in his pudgy, knuckle-less hand. Panic flares across her beautiful face as her cherry red lips part. She shakes her head, attempting to pull her arm away, and I'm already crossing the yard to them.

"I wouldn't do that if I were you, *Amico,*" Roman calls out, but I ignore him.

What the fuck else am I getting paid to do? Marco said keep unsavory characters away from his daughter and this asshole is the *most* unsavory of them all.

I swallow the distance between Sera and Deena. On my approach, Deena takes a step back, but he doesn't release her arm.

"Value your fingers, *Deena*?" I growl at him and he screws up his ugly, toad-like face, spitting on the tiles by my shoes.

"Who the fuck are you?"

I hate when people answer a question with a question. "Let her go and I'll gladly fill you in."

He tugs her closer to him, pressing the side of her body against his. "You don't know who you're talking to, boy."

Boy? How long has it been since I heard that one? "I don't give a shit who I'm talking to."

"Ben…" Sera's eyes are pleading, her lips pursed as she shakes her head, silently begging me to stop.

I may not be one of these…these…*made men*, but they should fear me all the same. With the right weapons, I could take them all out without breaking a Goddamn sweat.

"Ben?" Deena chuckles under his breath. "Well, *Ben*, you better get the fuck out of here before I—"

I draw my gun and point it right at his gigantic forehead. Adrenaline flurries through me, rushing through my blood with vigor and viscosity. I love it. The heaviness of metal and death in my hand. My finger twitches against the trigger and I want nothing more than to pull it and scatter his brains all

119

over the place.

Surrounding us, the clicks of guns being pointed in my direction—in every direction—signals a stalemate, but we have home court advantage.

"I'll ask you one more time. Do you value your fingers, *Deena?*" My finger twitches, begging to pull the trigger. "Because I'll gladly relieve you of them."

Deena glances around the yard with his beady, black eyes. He's looking for Ivan, probably, but what does he think Marco is gonna do when he walks out and sees him touching his precious, little girl? Me shooting his hand off will be the least of his worries.

Or maybe it won't be. I could have been wrong this whole time. Perhaps protecting his only daughter isn't as high on his priority list as I first assumed.

Deena flashes me his palm, dramatically releasing Sera's arm. "Happy?"

"Ecstatic," I deadpan. He attempts to push past me, but I lower my gun and snatch his soft elbow. "If I catch you within six feet of her again, I won't be so lenient."

Deena smiles widely, showcasing his crooked teeth. "You're a dead man."

He shrugs me off and I let him go, withdrawing my gun to my waistband. Behind me, Deena shouts for the guns to be put away before he storms into the house, disappearing from sight.

"Do I look like a damsel in distress to you?" Sera snaps, folding her arms across her chest.

I raise my eyebrows. "Wow. A simple thank you

would be nice."

"Thank you? He's going to kill you." She walks toward the orange juice fountain and I follow. "I can handle Deena. I've spent the last seven years of my life avoiding his awkward proposals. My father would never agree to it."

"You seem so certain."

"I am." Grabbing an empty glass from the stack, she fills it halfway and takes a small sip between her cherry lips before setting it down. "By the way, we need to go to the drug store."

I frown. "What for?"

"What do you mean what for?" she snaps in a whisper, swallowing a little distance. Her perfume engulfs me and she's close enough for me to assess her flawless make-up application. Subtle wings, a little highlighter, and long, black lashes that can't possibly be real. "Last night."

"Ssh." Licking my lips, I glance around us. Jesus. "I'm sure it's fine."

"And you want to risk it? If my father doesn't kill me for embarrassing the entire family with an illegitimate child, then you can explain why it has your eyes."

I roll my eyes. "You're not pregnant."

"No, I'm not." She picks up her glass again, her eyes skittering over my shoulder. "And I'd like to keep it that way. Hi, Daddy."

I turn around as Marco approaches, his thick, graying eyebrows pulled into a frown that makes me uneasy. "What the hell is going on out here, Ben? You're pulling guns on people like fucking Deena Giavanni? Have you lost your Goddamn mind?"

"I was doing my job," I tell him.

"Deena got grabby," Sera chimes in, cringing. "The usual."

Marco looks at Sera. "You all right?"

She nods, plastering on a fake, sad little pout. "I am thanks to Ben. I don't know what I would have done without him here."

I fight the urge to roll my eyes. She's overselling it. Like I said, she'd make a terrible actress.

"Fucking Deena," Marco spits, stuffing his hands into the pockets of his khaki slacks. "That useless pig. Do you know how insulting it is having to entertain this pack of fucking vermin? And at my place of rest, no less?"

At least we're both on the same level.

"I know Deena seems pushy with the nuptials, but unfortunately, there are offers I will have to consider soon."

Sera lowers her glass of orange juice, her face contorted as if it's the grossest thing she's ever tasted. "You've got to be kidding me."

"We've had this conversation a million times, Seraphina—"

I shift my weight. "You can't possibly be thinking about marrying her off to one of these…these—"

"—don't you open your mouth about somethin' you don't know," Marco snaps, and Sera storms off, her yellow summer dress bouncing around her thighs. "There's no man on this planet worthy of my daughter, but sometimes a father's gotta do what a father's gotta do to keep his family prospering.

Deena and his brother have made incredible offers for her hand time and time again. I can only refuse for so long and she's not helping. Have you heard the rumors?"

Clenching my jaw until my teeth hurt, I shake my head.

"The shit they say about my little girl…heartbreaking, truly fucking heartbreaking." He shrugs his shoulders. "Maybe throwing her into the deep end will help her sort her shit out."

I don't disagree. I don't agree, either. How can I? I open my mouth and I'm dead. I want to, though. I want to defend her, to tell him she's not as reckless as he thinks she is—and she's definitely not a whore. I've felt the inexperience in her touch. Sera's a good girl. A little lost, but still a good girl.

"I should go find Sera…"

Slapping a hand on my shoulder, Marco shakes his head. "No. She'll go to her room and cry for a few hours and then she'll be fine. In the meantime, I'll have James go home so she can't use the car and I'll put Roman on watch in the hall by her room."

Roman? That guy is just as twisted as Deena.

"And what would you rather have me do, then?"

"I have to leave for New York in a few hours and I need you to run a few errands for me."

Sounds fun, except I'm not his fucking errand boy. I clear my throat, careful not to display my displeasure. "All right."

***

It's late by the time I come back from running

Marco's errands. None of them were a part of my job description, but they weren't anything I couldn't handle. I did have to pistol whip an older gentleman for cash that he owed, but besides that, smooth sailing—with the exception of stopping at Walgreens for a "Plan B" morning after pill, of course. She's welcome to that. Christ. I don't even have ovaries and the woman at the counter made me feel terrible about buying one, silently judging me with her beady blue eyes.

I stalk up the stairs of the manor to a tired looking Roman, who drags on a cigarette as he leans his slender body against the front door. "What took you so long?"

I shrug. "It was a long list."

"You get it done?"

"Yeah."

He pushes off the door and drops down the stairs. "Good. I can go home."

I glance over my shoulder as I grab the door handle. "Who's here?"

"Seraphina and maybe Luca." He waves me off. "Why don't you have a Goddamn look?"

I open the door and go inside. I walk around the empty house looking for people, but I come up short. Eventually, I find myself outside of the two, huge double doors to Sera's room. I knock softly, but there's no answer. I call her name and she still ignores me.

"I got that thing you wanted…from Walgreens."

Nothing. Exhaling, I move to the wall opposite her door and I lean against it and wait.

For an hour, I wait and wait *and* wait, until I

can't take it anymore. I storm forward, grab the handle, and push the heavy door open. Her room is nothing like I expect. It's modern and sleek. There's even a fireplace and bookshelf filled with books—thick books.

I pause, scanning over everything, and I realize as I stare across the room and into a dark bathroom that she's not here.

"Sera?" I shout. "Where are you?"

No answer.

Fuck.

This is not happening.

CHAPTER ELEVEN

Sera

Late that night

I stand at the edge of the diving board, bouncing slightly with the wind. I've been standing here for a long time, staring into the pool, contemplating whether or not my so called "life" is worth living. I love my life, I do, but I loathe what's to become of it. Ivan's wife? Or worse, Deena's wife? I'd sooner shoot myself in the head. How could my father even contemplate imprisoning me to that life? Maybe I should bear Ben's child. No one would want to marry me then. My own father would be forced to disown me.

I toy with the handgun in my hand. It's heavier than I thought it'd be. I took it from the kitchen counter on my way out here. I don't plan on doing anything with it, I just…I don't know. I guess I wanted to see if I had what it takes to pull the trigger in the off chance that I'm married off to a

Giavanni.

I don't think I do.

After my parents left for New York, I walked—
no, I ran—to Naomi's place. She wasn't home,
naturally, but I knew where she kept her spare key. I
spent a long time there, waiting for her, but she
never showed up. After I called her a billion times,
she got back to me with a simple text saying she'd
call me later because she was out with the girls.

And I was alone.

I'd never envied her more than I did when I read
that text. She's free to do whatever, whenever.
She's free to marry whoever the hell she wants and
I'm…well, I'm me. A pawn to be married off in the
name of family.

When I came back, no one was home, no one
beside Luca, but even he had somewhere he needed
to be. I went to the guest house to talk to Ben, but
he was still out running my father's errands so, for
the first time in my life, I was free…and yet, I'd
never felt so isolated.

"Sera?"

My lips twitch as Ben's voice echoes around the
backyard, pulling me out of my thoughts.

"Come inside." The diving board I stand on
bounces and vibrates as he inches onto it. I hear him
shuffling toward me. "It's starting to rain."

I tilt my head back and tiny droplets of rain
patter over my face, growing larger and harder by
the second.

So it is.

The diving board begins to bend, lowering me
closer to the pool's surface, the nearer he gets to

me. I peer over my shoulder, ignoring droplets of water that cling to my lashes, and my heart skips a beat at the sight of his face. Relief and worry paint his expression, a beautiful mix on him.

Ben Campbell. The only part of today that I don't completely loathe.

I sigh and, suddenly, today doesn't feel so overwhelming. "Unzip me."

In the glow of the pool, his jaw tightens with impatience as his stare flickers to the gun in my hand. He doesn't want to unzip me. He wants me to hand over the weapon and go inside, but he doesn't open his mouth. Instead, he reaches for the zipper of my little yellow dress and drags it down. I lower one arm and the sleeve slides off, then I switch the gun in my hands and do the same with the other.

"I don't want to get the dress ruined," I say, letting the dress pool at my feet, parts of the fabric falling into the water anyway. The cool spattering of rain lands on my shoulders and my bare breasts. "I think you like this yellow one."

"Fuck the dress, Sera. Burn it. I don't care, just don't..." I flex my fingers against the gun as he speaks. "...just don't hurt yourself."

I slowly turn around and Ben—always the gentleman—keeps his stare on my face, not my chest.

"Why not?" I ask, tilting my head. "I don't want to marry Deena. Or Ivan."

"And you won't."

I see the promise in his eyes, the good intentions, but the problem is Ben doesn't know a damn thing about this way of life. About family, and honor, and deals. I was trade meat the second I was born. My father knew it. My mother knew it. And there's nothing Ben can do to change that, not even if he stepped up to marry me himself.

"I don't have a choice, if my father decides it." I extend the gun to Ben. "I wasn't going to do anything with this, anyway."

I don't have the courage. Cautiously, he reaches for the gun and quickly snatches it out of my hand before emptying it of its bullets and stuffing it into the back of his waistband. I look at his hand as he extends it to me with caution, as if I'm standing on the edge of an eight-story building.

"Let's go inside."

I shake my head. "I didn't come to the pool just to look at the water."

I jump off the diving board and crash into the water, kicking my legs to move to the far side of the pool.

When I come up for air, I peer at Ben, who stands on the board, his hands planted firmly on his hips. "Aren't you tired?" he shouts. "I'm tired."

I shake my head. "Go to sleep. I'm going to swim for a little bit."

Sighing, he glances up at the sky before lowering himself to sit on the board. I swim over to him and tread water to his left.

"I got you what you wanted from Walgreens." He reaches into his back pocket for a small packet. "And I never want to do it again."

"That bad, huh?"

I catch the words "emergency contraceptive" before he tears into it and pops a pill from its seal.

Moving over to the diving board, I grab the edge and lift myself up, opening my mouth. I stick out my tongue.

"Really?" he asks, giving me one of those famous "Ben" looks—the one with the furrowed brows and crinkles around his troubled eyes. He disapproves. Ben *always* disapproves.

I wiggle my eyebrows and he places the pill on my tongue with a sigh.

I swallow it, happily. "Thanks for that."

"Waste of money, if you ask me."

"I didn't ask you," I say. "Come in. The water's nice."

"I'm good."

Not taking no for an answer, I snag him by his shirt and I pull him into the pool. He curses as his large body breaks the surface, kicking his legs.

"Jesus Christ, Sera," he snaps. "You couldn't give me time to get my jacket off at least?"

I shrug, reaching for his shoulders. I curl my fingers around his jacket and push the soaking fabric halfway down his biceps. He treads water effortlessly as he shrugs his way out of his jacket and lets it sink to the bottom of the pool.

"Happy?" he asks and I smile at him.

He looks good wet. I like the way his hair shimmers with drops of water, flattening out his usual spiky, disheveled style. Above us, the clouds open up and the spattering of rain turns into a steady shower. The raindrops shimmer like diamonds in the glow of the pool as they descend before disappearing into the water.

"Do you swim topless often?"

"Only when I'm home alone." I laugh, inching closer to him. "I like to sunbathe naked too."

Swallowing, he averts his dark eyes across the yard.

"Are you blushing?" I tease, touching his chest.

"Don't be ridiculous."

His black button up shirt clings to his well-defined torso. I like touching him. I like the way he keeps his face so neutral, not betraying a single emotion. Ben Campbell has two personalities. Sometimes he's courteous and polite, the perfect guy to bring home to your mother. Other times, he's ruthless and reckless, filled with aggression and passion. I think of him as a masterpiece, a collection of intricate patterns that morph the longer you look at him. He's a complex human, that's for sure.

"Can I ask you a question?"

His eyebrows pull in and he settles his gaze on my face. "Preferably not."

"Do you like me?" I ask anyway, wrapping my legs around his waist so I no longer have to tread water.

I feel him tighten as I move my arms to bring my torso closer to his. I drape my arms around his neck and he *still* manages to keep both our heads above water.

"Do I like you?" He nods, averting his eyes. "Sure. I like you. You're a good girl."

"No." I squeeze him tighter. "Do you *like* me?"

I imply everything in my tone. *Do you like me romantically? Sexually?*

Ben takes his time to answer my question and his face, the face that so easily masks his emotions, betrays him as he ponders.

"Yeah..." he mutters after an eternity. "I *like* you."

Grinning, I brush my lips against his mouth, kissing him gently. He allows it, even reciprocates with his full lips, but he cuts it short, using one hand to unwrap my legs from his body.

"But I'm a lot older than you, Sera. You have your whole life to—"

He cuts his sentence short and I go back to treading water as Ben moves away from me, retreating underneath the diving board, like I'm some kind of sick animal.

"Deena is a forty-six-year old man," I point out, swimming closer, and it occurs to me that I've never asked Ben his age.

His skin is fresh, a little weathered in some places, but it only adds to this rugged appeal he's got going on. I just assumed it's from his time in the army.

"How old are you?" I ask.

Ben grips the diving board in his hands and stops kicking his legs. I grab the other side and hang in front of him.

"You don't know how old I am?"

I shake my head. "Twenty-seven? Twenty-eight?"

He smirks. "Thirty-two."

"Oh."

"Yeah, *oh*."

"I didn't mean it like *that*." I pull myself closer to him, letting go of the board. "I don't mind your age."

"Good to know."

He moves away, swimming backward toward the steps. I notice, as I swim out from underneath the diving board, that the rain has stopped.

"Why are you running from me?" I demand, placing my feet against the bottom of the pool and standing up. The water laps at my ribs, my nipples instantly hardening in the cold breeze. "You've known my age for weeks and last night you still—"

"—I don't want to talk about last night," he snaps, sitting on the stairs, his lower half still submerged in water.

I fold my arms across my chest. "Because you're embarrassed?"

"Because it will never happen again."

I flinch. Never? "I thought you had a good time?"

"I did." He pushes five thick fingers through his hair, sending water spraying in different directions. "I did, but...I don't think I like where this is heading."

I lower my head and peer into the water. He doesn't have to explain it. I know exactly what he means. This doesn't end well. We can never date each other. We can never have a normal relationship—not that a relationship is something I'm chasing.

"Sneaking around is not how I envisioned my love life at thirty," he admits. "Yeah, it's exciting for you because *I'm* the older guy your parents would never, ever approve of, but I'm the person who's supposed to protect you, to stop you from doing what you're doing. I'm not supposed to be the guy who runs out and buys you morning after pills because *I* couldn't control myself—because *I* couldn't keep my word to your father."

I step forward, lifting my eyes to him. "We started before my father came into the picture."

"It was a one-night stand," he counters, pissing me off.

It might have just been a one-night stand to him, but it was more than that for me. It was an act of freedom, the first time in a long time that I've made a decision for *myself* for a change. "Yeah, and now it isn't."

"You should stay away from me, Sera."

"I should." I move closer, placing one foot on the bottom step. "But I'm not going to." I slip right into his lap, pressing my chest against his, my lips twitching when he makes no effort to fight me off. "I'm glad you came into my life. You're the only one I can truly be myself around."

Smoothing my hands over his chest, I brush my mouth against his, kissing the corner of his lips. He doesn't pull away and I shiver as the wind continues to blow, inciting goosebumps all over my body.

"We could be great together," I utter, toying with his top button.

It opens and I move to the second, then the third, exposing his beautiful, tan chest. Like mine, his skin is covered in tiny, cold little goosebumps, but neither of us seem to be affected by the weather.

"Or we could be a disaster," he grumbles back, watching my lips with hooded eyes.

For a man as strong looking as Ben, he sure doesn't hide that women—or perhaps a particular *woman*—is his weakness. I crush my mouth to his, sliding my tongue inside. He kisses me back, his hands flying to my body, touching me all over. I break this kiss with a groan as he palms my breasts and kisses my neck, devouring every inch of it.

"We can make this work...you and me?" I sigh, raking my fingers through his hair as he noisily sucks at my breasts. "We could run away together. See the world."

Exhaling, he pulls his mouth from my skin and slides his forehead against mine. "Sounds like something two crazy people in love would do."

"We could fall in love along the way," I say, grabbing at his sleek belt buckle. "Stranger things have happened."

"I suppose they have."

Ben leans back, bracing himself with his elbows on the final step behind him as I undo his belt, lower his zipper and pull his pants wide enough for his hard, thick cock to spring free. My breath hitches as it juts up at me, standing so proudly. Licking my lips, I lean forward, pushing it between my legs. Groaning, Ben sits forward and reaches around me, pulling my pathetic, lace panties to the side and pushing my lower back with the other hand. I bite my lower lips and settle gently against the very tip of him, preparing to take him inside. Only he forces me down with a loud grunt, roughly shoving his cock inside of me. I gasp in euphoric shock, arching my back and digging my nails into his chest, drawing blood.

Ben kisses me and, surprisingly, it's a much slower pace than what I was expecting. I close my eyes as he smooths his hands up my body and into the nape of my neck. Just like that, my body enlivens with erotic sensations. He kisses me harder, then, making slow movements with his hips that force the tip of his cock against my cervix. It's uncomfortable and absolutely amazing all at once.

I'm ready for him to unleash on me, to take me places only he's been able to take me, but a ringing in the distance pulls us from our lust-induced stupor.

"Shit." Ben curses. "That's my phone."

"Where is it?"

He grabs my hips and slips out of me. "On the grass. I thought I was going to have to dive in after you."

I swing my leg over him and move to the left, sitting on the step as he rushes from the pool, stuffing himself back into his pants. Dripping wet, he answers his cell just in time and removes the empty gun from his waistband.

"Hello? Marco, hi."

I roll my eyes and adjust my underwear, covering myself up.

"Yes. Everything is fine…she was swimming. Now? Now she's inside. Yes. All right…okay." He hangs up and rakes his fingers through his hair. "Your father is at JFK, getting ready to board his flight back here."

I shrug. "Okay?"

Ben taps his phone in his palm, blowing air out of his cheeks. "Put your dress back on, Sera. Go to bed."

Exhaling, I drop my head back and look at the

sky. I want to protest him, but what's the point? I stand up and ascend the stairs, clenching my body to protect myself from the cold. It doesn't work, obviously. I ditch my dress altogether and head toward the house, bypassing Ben on the way.

"You're not going to take your dress?" he shouts after me and I wave him off, too embarrassed to collect my things.

It's funny how that works. How sex has a way of making you so vulnerable and the smallest thing becomes such a big issue. Eleven feet out from the back door, my teeth begin to chatter and being in the water is something I start to regret.

"Well, well, well," I freeze with a gasp as Deena and two of his men come out of nowhere. He sneers at me, his ugly face contorting in anger and absolute delight. "It's no wonder Ben Campbell came to your rescue. You're his little whore."

I take a minute step back, shielding my breasts. Deena storms forward and I scream, turning my body. "Ben!"

Wham! For a split of a second, my skull feels like it cracks in half...

...then darkness swallows me.

CHAPTER TWELVE

Ben

Water hits my face, a familiar sensation, only this time it's enough to make my eyelids flutter.

It's a peculiar phenomenon, losing a chunk of your life to something other than sleep, something forceful. Blowing air from my cheeks and excess water from my lips, I shiver, finally opening my eyes.

"Where…?" I blink and clench my jaw against the pain in the back of my skull that radiates down my neck. "What…?"

"Look who decided to wake up," someone says.

I blink rapidly, desperate to clear the blur that coats my eyes, but I can't put a face to the voice, no matter how hard I try.

What's the last thing I remember? Swimming…

Sera…

Her blood chilling scream…

Deena.

Then nothing.

I close my eyes as blackness closes in around the edges, threatening to pull me back under.

"Oh, no you don't. I've wasted an entire day waiting for you to wake up."

Another rush of water washes over my face and I gasp, lifting my head despite the pain in my neck. The water is freezing. I'm alert enough now to feel it down to my bones. I shake my head repeatedly, unable to free my arms from behind my back. I blink again and again, before finally, the lines of the world sharpen. Rope burns my wrists and my shoulders ache from being strapped to the chair like this.

"He's awake."

I turn my head with a wince toward the voice, toward Roman who leans against a dodgy pipe, smoking a damn cigarette.

Where am I? I take in the hot water tanks and the semi-extensive piping system. I must be in a basement. Marco's basement. It has to be.

"Where is she?"

I drag my attention to the man himself who sits in front of me, perched on a stool brandishing gold plated brass knuckles. *Fuck.* Marco's face is placid, betraying no emotion, no panic. I take in his khaki slacks and black polo, a handgun jutting out of his waistband.

I'm going to die here.

"I...I don't know."

He shoots off his stool and hits me in the face, sparing me the brass by using his left hand. His knuckles collide with my jaw, throwing it out of alignment and tossing my head to the side. I groan

139

as the pain spreads over my entire face and down my spine.

"What'd you do with her?" he snaps, and I pull my head back.

"What did *I* do with her?" Is he serious? "I didn't do a damn thing."

"No?" He whirls on his heel and opens a gray plastic bag. Inside it, he pulls out Sera's soaking yellow dress, and my jacket to match. "These were found in the pool. *Together,*" he points out. "Care to explain?"

Oh, shit. I look him dead in the eyes. "It's not what you think."

He raises an eyebrow and it's disbelieving. "It's not?"

"No. After running your errands, I came home to find Sera in the pool—her dress cast to the side." It's not a complete lie, it's just an altered storyline. An alternative fact. "I thought something was wrong, so I dove in after her. That's all."

Marco tosses the clothes to the floor with a stomp of his foot. "And Luca, one of my loyalist men, who claimed to see you fucking my daughter, is a liar?"

"Luca?" I spit. I checked the entire house before Sera went missing. No one was home. "Bullshit. I didn't touch her."

My stomach sinks into my shoes...I don't have access to every room in the house. Luca could've been there. Or he could have shown up while I was distracted by Sera. How was I to know?

"And the shopping you did at Walgreens? That has nothing to do with *my* Sera?"

It had everything to do with her. I pull against my ropes, spitting water onto the concrete at my feet. Wait. How does he know I went to Walgreens?

"Have you been following me?"

"I don't know who the fuck you are. Of course, I've been following you." He rubs his left hand, the one he hit me with, massaging each knuckle. "You think I'm just gonna let some man I found on the street into my daughter's life without observing him first?"

He goes on for a while and I expect him to bring up the first night I spent at his house. The night Sera snuck into my place. How can I deny that night?

Thankfully, as he finishes up his speech about killing a man named Leo in this very spot for betraying him and his daughter, I realize he isn't going to bring the first night up. He has no idea what we got up to while he slept soundly in his bed.

"Whatever Luca claims happened between Sera and I isn't true," I tell him, praying to a damn God I don't believe in that there's no physical evidence. "Deena has her, Marco, and she's in a lot of trouble. Let me help."

He whips the gun from his waistband and presses the barrel to my forehead. "Swear to me."

Little bubbles of sweat form on my head and above my lip, but he can't tell. "Swear to you about—"

"—about fucking my daughter. If you didn't, swear to me."

I'm going to hell anyway. What's one more mark against my name?

"I swear to you...I have *never* laid a finger on

your daughter."

Marco clenches his jaw on and off repeatedly. "If I find out you're lying to me—"

"—I'll stay away," I interrupt. "If you don't trust me, fine, I'll quit and I'll stay away, just let me help you with this."

He thinks about it. He thinks about it long enough for his phone to ring. Without lowering the gun, without taking his eyes off me, he reaches into his pocket with his brass dusted hand and takes the call.

"Deena…" Marco greets him and my blood drains to my shoes. "Rumor has it you have something that belongs to me."

I stare back at Marco and watch his coal eyes darken even further, if that's possible. His usual tan complexion slowly turns red before he explodes.

"I'm going to cut your fucking head off!" he screams into the phone. Veins pop up on his forehead as spit flies in all directions. "How dare you betray me, you cunt! I will end you! I will *fucking* end you!"

I sit still, my body tightly coiled, as Marco tears away from me and slams his phone against a concrete wall, smashing it into pieces.

"Marco—"

He swings at me with his right hand and I grunt as the metal strapped to his knuckles rips through my skin, splitting my cheek and my lip. "You lied to me, you piece of shit!"

I groan, hanging limply against the rope. Breathing through my nose, I spit blood against the wet floor. When I'm certain I can take another hit if

I have to, I lift my head. I betrayed him. The least I can do is look him in the eye. "Yeah, I did."

Clenching his teeth, he pulls his fist back and lets it fly, hitting me again. I growl in pain as the pointed metal knuckles tear my skin apart. I close my eyes, trying my hardest to ignore the way my brain spins in my skull. He's going to kill me.

I'm going to die here.

Marco whistles and Roman crosses the room to stand behind me. Grabbing a fistful of my hair, he holds me upright, to face the consequences of my actions. I open my eyes. "I met her...I met her before I started the job. She was the reason I didn't want it in the first place."

He hits me again and I survive it, somehow.

"Marco, *fuck!* What else do you want me to say?"

My face is swollen, my lips refusing to move the way my brain tells them to. Roman releases me, and my head sags. I watch blood as it drips onto my lap and seeps into the fabric of my pants.

"Do whatever you want to me, but don't judge her. She's a good girl." I spit and fail, it dribbles off my lips and down my chin. "She just wants to enjoy her life."

Marco snatches a fistful of my hair and yanks my head back. I hiss as he comes face to face with me.

"We're going to get her back. After that, I don't want to see your face around Vegas again, understood?"

I swallow hard, and all I taste is blood and metal. I do my best to nod, but he's not happy with it.

"I asked you a damn question."

"I…I…" Blood coagulates in my throat, making it harder to speak. "Understand."

"Good." He drops my head and Roman cuts the ropes that constrict my arms. Groaning, I fall forward, crashing to the concrete…

…then I die.

***

I float back into consciousness by the motion of the vehicle as it speeds down a sandy track. I groan as I straighten my back. Fortunately, I'm not dead. Unfortunately, I feel like I've been hit by a truck. What a fucking night.

I haven't felt this beat up since I was kidnapped and tortured by the Taliban in oh-nine. They beat me within an inch of my life, among other shit I don't want to recall at the moment.

Marco sits in the passenger seat, grumbling orders at the guy driving, a guy I've never seen before. To be honest, I'm in no fucking state for this shit. My nerves wage war. Sickness churns in my stomach over and over, causing a clammy sweat to bloom across the surface of my skin.

I have to do this.

I should have been watching, instead, I was lulled into the false sense of security her house provided—that her body provided. I pissed Deena off. A fucking mob member. Of course, he's gonna want revenge. How fucking stupid can I be?

I push off of the door and tug my seatbelt, loosening it.

"You're an idiot, you know," Roman utters beside me and I turn my head with a wince.

"Yeah, I know."

He slaps a handgun in the palm of my hand as the car rolls to a stop and the men climb out. I do my best to unclip my seatbelt and then open the door. Everything I do makes my body scream, but I push on regardless, swinging my legs over the edge of the seat and out of the car.

I drop onto the sand beneath my feet with a grunt and step forward as more cars pull up behind us.

"Deena!" Marco shouts and I lift my head to see the mansion before me. "Where are you, you fucking coward?"

Loud pings surround us as bullets rain down, hitting the cars, causing sparks to skitter. Adrenaline hits me, it rushes through my blood and picks me up better than any methamphetamine I've never tried. I rush round the rear of our SUV, my chest heaving as I press my back harder against the metal. This has got to be the stupidest thing I've ever done for a girl.

Roman joins me, cradling his handgun to his chest.

"Fucking madness!" he shouts. "Christ!

I turn to him.

"I need a rifle!" I yell over the ruckus.

He flicks his head to the car we hide behind. "In the bag on the floor."

Stuffing my handgun into my pocket, I pull open the rear door and reach for the bag on the floor. *Crash!* The window opposite me is blown out and I keep my head down as the glass rains down on me.

I just manage to get the bag open and the rifle out when I hear the words: "Grenade launcher!"

"Shit!"

I turn and run like I've never run before. I run like I'm healthy, like I'm not at death's door. The dune of sand in front of me becomes steep, so I scurry on my hands and feet to get over the top. A whistle pierces the silent night and I use the last of my strength to dive over the top.

"Unh!" I land on my back, air forced from my lungs, followed by an explosion big enough to alert every authority figure in the state.

I can't believe this all started because I couldn't keep my hands off a peculiar girl I met in a club.

I roll onto my stomach and cover my head as debris pelts down like hail.

I knew she'd be the worst kind of trouble. I fucking knew it.

When it stops, I grab my rifle and peer over the top of the dune. I see the mansion clearly and the men that stand at the front. Closing one eye, I prop my rifle on the dune, placing the butt against my shoulder, and I look down the Nightforce scope to get a better look.

I see the guy with the launcher. I watch as he dumps the portable M72 one-shot and is handed another one. Where the fuck did these people get these kinds of weapons?

Regardless, I have to stop him. I line him up in my scope and hold my breath, hoping to slow my heart. I wasn't a sniper in the army. Sure, I had minor training, but it wasn't my specialty. Lucky for me, I'm not shooting from a crazy distance.

I squeeze the trigger and his head is splattered across the gate behind him. He crashes to the floor and the rest of his buddies drop like flies.

Unscathed, I see Marco's men rush the gates, Marco in tow. I force myself to my feet and rush through the sand, dodging chunks of metal and angry flames.

When I catch up, Marco eyes me sideways. "Nice shot."

I flick my shoulder. "Thanks."

"I still fucking hate you."

"Good to know."

Jogging beside him, one of Marco's men takes Marco's handgun and replaces it with a machine gun. "Open up the fucking gates, before I blast them off their hinges."

We wait in the silence, but nothing happens. To the left, Roman takes a phone call and begins swearing his ass off in Italian before tossing the phone to Marco.

"What?" he answers, pointing his machine gun to the sky. "I don't care, Ivan. I'm going to decapitate your brother and send you his Goddamn head! Oh, you're threatening me with war? I'm already at the battlefront, you dead-eyed, motherfucking, ugly son of a—" Roaring, he tosses the phone against the cobblestone at his feet, breaking it. "Deeeeenaaaa!"

Slinging my rifle over my shoulder, I move toward the headless body with the rocket launcher and scoop it up. "Get back!"

I rush back a few feet before letting the bad bitch loose. The metal warms in my hand as she ignites and blows the gates to smithereens, slamming metal into a handful of Deena's Lamborghinis parked along the drive. If I could smile with these nerve dead lips, I'm sure I would.

Grabbing my rifle, I rake my fingers through my hair and push forward. It doesn't take us long to enter the huge establishment through the front door.

Inside is immaculate, oddly royal, and extremely quiet. Too quiet.

Then, they come out of the woodwork like the maggots they are. We scatter, diving behind marble columns and whatever fortified furnitures we can find. I take out as many as I can before my gun jams, rendering itself useless. I toss it to the side and grab the handgun from my damp waistband.

"Daddy?" a feminine voice pierces through the madness and my ears prick at the sound.

"She's upstairs!" I shout at Marco, who shoots from behind the thick column beside mine. "If you go right, I'll go left."

He nods at me before rushing to the next column. I go the opposite way, moving toward the staircase that curls around from each side, but meets in the middle.

I shout, demanding Marco's men lay down some suppressive fire, but none of them know what the hell it even means, so I risk my own ass. I rush the stairs with only my handgun and two bullets remaining, using them both to kill the last two of Deena's men. I throw my handgun to the floor and snatch a rifle from the dead body of the man at my feet.

Marco joins up with me a minute later, out of

breath.

"Get the door," he says to Roman and we stand out of the way.

Roman shrugs out of his jacket and inches up to the door, clenching a double barrel shotgun in his hand. I hold my breath as he slowly turns the handle and yanks the door open.

Marco rushes inside and his men follow without instruction. I wait, patiently, and the sounds of Marco losing his damn mind again is all the information I need to know.

Deena is in the room.

And the girly sobs that manage to seep through the mess and penetrate my soul tells me that so is Sera.

CHAPTER THIRTEEN

Sera

Deena holds me against his hard, chubby body, his handgun pressed to my temple as we stand behind his large wood grain desk littered with papers and God knows what else. I'm dressed in only a gray t-shirt much too large for me. The neckline of the shirt sags over my shoulder, threatening to expose my left breast to my father and his minions.

In the group that huddles by the large, oak double doors with their guns pointed in our direction, I see a lot of familiar faces except for the only one I really want to see. I gasp. What if Dad hurt him? What if he's…I don't want to think about it.

"I'm going to skin you alive, Deena," my father growls, inching closer.

"Come any closer and I'll blow her brains out."

I swallow hard.

"You dumb fuck," my dad swears. "I was

considering your offer in exchange for her hand. You couldn't wait a few weeks? You had to swoop in while I was away?"

Deena laughs and it vibrates against my back. "I didn't go to your house for her. I came for the fucker that insulted me, the one that put a gun to my head," I hear him sneer, right by my ear. "But when I saw them in the pool, all over each other, I thought I was doing you a favor by taking this whore off your hands. Free of charge."

Dad flinches, clenching his jaw harder than I've ever seen. Tears well in my eyes as he looks at me not only with fear and anger, but disappointment too. It pierces my heart.

My soul.

If only he knew that Ben is a good man. He's not like Deena. He's not like anyone else I've ever met.

"If you've got a problem with me, Deena, let the girl go and we can talk."

The tears that well in my eyes dry up and my chest inflates with hope. I watch my father's group slowly branch out, Ben coming into the room from behind them, a rifle pressed against his shoulder. I gasp at the sight of him. His mouth bleeds, his eye almost swollen shut. My chest aches, the tears coming back full force. What'd they do?

"The time for talking is over," Deena snaps in my ear, startling me. "I kill her or I kill you."

I glance down at the desk in front of me, spotting a gold envelope opener on the edge. I'd question why the hell anyone would still use one of these, but fuck it. Men like Deena thrive on nostalgia.

"Tell me, Ben. Is her pussy so good you'd give

your life for it?"

Ben grimaces—or I think he does. It's hard to tell under all that blood. "Stop talking."

Glancing down, I slowly reach for the envelope opener. Grabbing it by its blade, I pull it back and hold it by its hilt. His chest vibrates as he talks, but I can't hear him. All I can hear is my heart as it pounds in my ears. I moisten my lips and clench the envelope opener. I exhale, then inhale. All I gotta do is drive this into his thigh muscle and run. I lift the opener as high as I can without alerting Deena to what I'm doing. I close my eyes for the briefest moment and pray to God that he doesn't squeeze the trigger on reflex.

Clenching my teeth together, I slam the envelope opener into Deena's thigh and he howls in pain.

Bang! I dive out of the way, crying out as my hip slams into the hard wood when I crash to the floor. *Bang.*

There's a ringing in my ears I can't seem to shake. I stuff them with my fingers, and I remain still, squeezing my eyes shut. Hands grab at me—all different kinds of hands—and they pull me to my feet. I open my eyes as my father's men drag me toward the door. I watch the scene before me unfold in slo-mo. Deena cradles his shoulder on the floor, his face red, dribbling spit out of his mouth while he unintelligibly yells at my father, who towers above him.

To his left, Roman, Luca, and Levi stand above Ben, stomping their feet all over him. Screaming, I thrash against the men that hold me and manage to slip free.

My father moves toward Ben before I'm close enough to stop him.

"Dad, no!" I cross the floor, rushing over to him. Pulling back his leg, he kicks Ben in the ribs. Ben curls up with a groan, clenching his body tightly.

"Daddy, please!"

I force my way between them and kneel at Ben's side, exposing my palms to my father, tears burning hot trails down my cheeks.

"Get out of my way," he demands, flicking his head at Luca, who grabs my arms and tugs me to my feet.

I dig my feet in, no longer able to see the sharp lines of my father's angry face. I beg him over and over to leave Ben alone. In a panic, I promise to never speak to Ben again. I promise to never leave the house. I promise to marry whoever he wants me to marry so long as Ben is spared.

"It's not his fault," I shout, a few feet from the room's exit. "He didn't do anything! I did." I hiccup, wincing as my lungs and my throat burn. "He saved my life! And you're not going to spare him?"

I'm tugged out of the room and the door is slammed shut in my face. I sag in Luca's grip as all my fight leaves my body. I knew this would happen. I fucking knew it would…

…and still I persisted.

Ben

Once the last of my adrenaline is kicked out of me, my body gives up. I hear them shout above me, but I don't have the energy to fully process the words they speak. Only once voice stands out above the fray, *hers.*

I hear it, but it grows more and more distant, and the further it fades, the less I want to stay here.

"At least let me call him an ambulance." Her cry echoes through my head, and I can't muster the energy to tell her I'm okay.

I hear faint murmurs of Marco as he demands they take Deena to "the warehouse" for his punishment and I wonder if that's where I'll end up.

It's funny. I went from complaining because the jobs I was doing weren't exciting enough to working as a bodyguard for some mafia princess. And now I'm lying on the floor of a mob's mansion, minutes away from death because of a fucking girl I met at a club I didn't even want to be at. Sera and I were destined to fail from the beginning, really. The sex was just too good for us to see the bigger picture.

My eyelids grow heavy, so heavy I don't think I can open them ever again…

…man, my brother is going to be pissed when he finds out I couldn't even keep this job for longer than two days, but hey, at least I tried.

EPILOGUE

Ben

Months later

I suck the last of my chocolate milkshake up the long, red and white straw, uncaring that it makes that annoying slurping sound people hate so much. I feel their stares on me and imagine their eyebrows pulling tightly together as their frustrations mount.

The milkshakes are mediocre today. They were the best once.

I pick up my napkin and swipe it once across my lips before scrunching it in my fist and dropping it into the tall, empty glass. Exhaling, I slide out of the spacious, red leather booth and pull my wallet out of the back pocket of my worn jeans. The milkshakes here didn't always cost six dollars. I swear they hike the price up every time I come.

Bastards.

I drop a twenty-dollar bill on the table and turn toward the exit.

"See you tomorrow, Ben."

I don't look at the waitress, Donna, as I saunter past the counter where she pours a young gentleman in clean, denim overalls a fresh, hot coffee.

"See you tomorrow, Donna."

Bells clash together as I press my palm to the door of the isolated little roadhouse on the edge of town and step outside. Warm summer air kisses my face and I sigh.

It's a good day to be alive.

The recovery from the beating I took was a long road. I spent a few solid weeks in the hospital and an extra few at Chad's place as he helped nurse me back to health. When I was ready, I called my brother and I apologized for complaining about working an average job. I promised I'd give it my all if he gave me another chance and he did. The only good thing to come out of my brief time working for the Ventillis was the fact Marco paid off my mother's house as thanks for helping him save Sera. No words were exchanged, just a note that said:

"Consider this payment for your two days. –Marco."

Which brings me to now.

My name is Ben Campbell, I'm a full blooded American, and I no longer serve in the United States Army. Instead, I fetch coffee and mix concrete, but I don't get shot at and, after the last eleven years of my life, that's all I can ask for.

I never left Vegas, even though Marco demanded

it the night everything went to shit. I figured if he wanted to kill me, he would have already. Besides, I'm not leaving my mother's house. She loved it more than anything.

Stomping down the metal stairs in my heavy, brown boots, I reach into the front pocket of my jeans and pluck out a fresh, full packet of cigarettes. Flicking the cardboard flap back, I take out a cigarette and pinch it between my lips. I move toward my big black truck, resting against its bull bar, bending my leg at the knee. I pluck the cigarette from my lips and glance down at it.

I don't even feel like having it. I stuff it into the back pocket of my jeans and push off my truck.

Behind me, the sounds of gravel crushing underneath the tires of a car get awfully close. I turn around and my heart drops into my intestines at the sight of a sleek, black town car, the number plate reading a surname I never thought I'd see again.

Ventilli.

I wait with bated breath before the rear passenger door opens and out steps Marco, wearing a black polo and matching slacks.

Fuck. I fold my arms across my chest. What the hell did I do now? If he's here to demand I leave, he's in for a rude awakening. He'll have to kill me.

Pursing his lips, Marco steps to the side and flicks his head at whoever is inside. My lips part when I see her bounce out wearing a cute blue summer dress that doesn't expose her cleavage, but cuts off high above the knee. Her long, wavy black hair curls around her breasts and she beams widely at me, so wide her cheeks look like they're about to pop, but holy shit is she as beautiful as ever.

Marco turns to me and my heart races. "If you want to see my daughter, then we need to lay down some ground rules, all right?"

I open my mouth and a pathetic rush of air comes out. I just…I just can't believe I'm laying my eyes on her. Right now. In the flesh.

"Swing by the house this evening and we can have a chat."

Marco mutters something to Sera before lowering himself into the car. I watch the car drive off, leaving me alone with her.

Alone.

For the first time since that awful night.

"Hi," she says when the dust settles, smiling sweetly at me.

"Hi." I shake my head, still in shock. "You look good."

Blush swells in her cheeks and she glances down at her thin strapped sandals. "So do you."

The air between us feels like it should be awkward, but it isn't. I just don't know where to start. I scratch my head. If I knew I was going to see her today, I would have put more effort into my appearance. I would have shaved this stubble and ran a comb through my hair. I look like shit. Worn jeans and a grey tee covered in faint white powder from a hard day's work.

I grab my baseball cap at the front and lift it to nervously scratch at my hair. "This isn't a test, is it?"

She steps closer, placing her hands behind her back. "You haven't touched me yet so, if it was, you've passed with flying colors."

Holy fuck, I've missed her. I pull off my cap and open my arms to her. Grinning widely, she rushes toward me and throws her small body against mine. Inhaling her sweet scent, I lift her off the ground and hug her tightly. She cups my face and plants a long kiss on my mouth. I close my eyes and pray this isn't a dream. She smiles against my lips and her touch doesn't fade away, like it does most nights. She's here. She's in my arms, and this time it's not sordid or something I should be ashamed of. For the first time in a long time, this place finally feels like home.

I melt into Sera as three little words come to mind.

God bless America.

THE END

Acknowledgements

Thank you to my husband, my two girls, and my newborn son. I love the four of you to the moon and back. Always. Thank you for your never-ending patience.

To Limitless Publishing, who continues to publish me even though I've slowed down these past few years. Your loyalty means the world to me.

As always, a huge, huge thank you to my editor, and friend, Toni, who takes all of my rough manuscripts and sprinkles her magic! I appreciate everything you do for me and my work.

To my crew in Madi's Minxes, thank you for liking, commenting, and sharing my excerpts, my teasers, and my new releases. Your excitement keeps me going.

Lastly, thank you to my readers—wait and wait! You will get the books I've promised you soon.

About the Author

Skyla Madi was born in the small town of Port Maquarie, New South Wales in 1993. She spent half her life growing up in Wauchope, a thriving rural town at the heart of the Hastings River Valley before making the leap to the busy city of Brisbane.

Whenever this young Australian writer isn't changing diapers, watching cartoons, cooking for her husband or doing other motherly-wife things she is actively working on her writing and improving her writing skills.

Facebook:
https://www.facebook.com/SkylaMadi

Twitter:
https://twitter.com/Skyla_Madi

Website:
http://skylamadiauthor.wix.com/skylamadi

Goodreads:
http://www.goodreads.com/author/show/6554179.S
kyla_Madi